Unimportant
People

At the beginning of the war there was enthusiasm.
At the end of the war there was hope.
Fifteen years later, there was despair.

Unimportant
People

At the beginning of the war there was enthusiasm.
At the end of the war there was hope.
Fifteen years later, there was despair.

Zorica Kecojevic

Published in Australia by Zoro Publishing
First published in Australia 2017
Copyright © Zorica Kecojevic 2017
Email: zoricakec@gmail.com

National Library of Australia Cataloguing–in–Publication entry
Creator: Kecojevic, Zorica,
Title, Author: Unimportant people, Zorica Kecojevic.
ISBN: 978-0-6480948-0-7 (paperback)
ISBN: 978-0-6480948-1-4 (ebook)
Subjects: War and society--Fiction.
                  Bosnians--Fiction.
                  Immigrants--Fiction.
                  Yugoslav War, 1991-1995--Fiction.
                  Bosnia--Fiction.

Cover photography by Zorica Kecojevic
Cover design and typesetting by Nelly Murariu, PixBeeDesign.com
Printed by IngramSpark

Disclaimer
All care has been taken in the preparation of the information herein, but no responsibility can be accepted by the publisher or author for any damages resulting from the misinterpretation of this work.

"This book is dedicated to all the people of Bosnia living around the world and the ones still remaining there. With all my love and loyalty to my sister and nephew. With my deepest love to my mother."

Introduction

Unimportant People is a fictional book that has a strong sense of authenticity. It is a story of several people who each leave ex-Yugoslavia in the early 1990s due to the war starting in Bosnia and Herzegovina. They move to different countries around the world in search of a better life. The story also follows some who stay in Bosnia during the conflict. Who is better off?

The sense of family and old roots are strong, but the quest for a better life includes abandoning some, if not all, of their traditions and embracing new ones.

The story is about six different characters, who are not dissimilar to ordinary people we meet in everyday life. Some of them are followed in their struggle in a new country while other characters are accompanied in their misfortunes through the war in Bosnia.

This is a simple story of love, friendships, youth and old age. It is a story about war and everyday life, what the war brings, and how much it takes. Some readers might find deeper meaning beyond the pages of this book, but some may not. Neither will be at a loss as a result.

CHAPTER I

Melbourne, Australia, 2000s

In the background, she could hear words of a song: *'Did I disappoint you; leave a bad taste in your mouth?'*

There was a bad taste, bad feeling, heavy feeling in Tanya that would not lift, that would not go away. She was trembling at the thought, she felt dizzy. She felt soiled, dirtied. The half-witted creature she went out with the night before had left a wet, slobber of a kiss on her cheek at the end.

'I'll call ya,' he'd yelled after her.

No, do not call me, Tanya thought. *I do not want to hear any more of your 'dreams' in life and needs unfulfilled at the age of forty-plus. I feel bad enough without you.*

After she had driven home that night, she'd promised herself never again would she try Internet dating. It was not the right thing for her.

Still, the day after, as all her feelings of inadequacy flooded back, she was overwhelmed by a strong sense of repulsion. She was sickeningly aware of herself, of her raw, almost animalistic needs, and thought that everybody else could see into her mind, like a display screen with clearly written description of how low and unloved she felt.

She tried to put a smile on her face while gliding among groups of people pretending to be busy. She could not comprehend what role was she supposed to play, or what her life was all about. This waitressing job was only temporary, and all the hard work to get her degree seemed futile as she held a tray whilst performing a smile. A stranger might tell her to hold on and that she couldn't find a job in her field of education as she only recently immigrated. Be patient.

Something will come up. There's a job out there with your name on it. A major in Serbian language was not going to get her far in the country where the main language was English. Finding a job was just one of the hurdles.

'Hello, having fun?' Lauren smiled at her.

She could not figure out Lauren's smile. It seemed Lauren made a special effort to smile, to stretch the corners of her lips upward and show two rows of perfect white teeth. Lauren resembled a bull terrier, ready to jump if attacked, or if someone dared to take a bone off her. Still, people liked Lauren and Tanya saw that as yet another mystery. Not that she was jealous of Lauren's popularity, but it was just puzzling: what makes a person popular?

Tanya never wanted to be popular or 'LIKED'. Waste of time. Or maybe not? Maybe that was the root of her problems – a lack of sense of purpose. Maybe she could be nicer to people, smile more and be kinder, to a point – stop before feeling used, and then in that way create a good atmosphere around herself.

That worked until somebody threw her off balance with a snide remark. How did you keep yourself above that? *There are so many rules in life, and there is not one book that puts them all together like a Readers Digest.*

She stood by one table and watched a woman sipping her white wine. Through the large, floor-to-ceiling window, Tanya saw her reflection. She had intensely brown hair, now lifted into a bun, dark eyes and reasonably reasonably straight nose; a slim, athletic build. Still, Tanya did not like her own look, so she shifted her gaze outward.

The function room was on the 18th floor of a corporate building, and the view of the city and the bay beyond was magnificent.

There were twenty-odd tables scattered around the large room, and while two of the walls were bare, the third was almost all glass, revealing a beautiful sunny day outside. Large white houses snuggled around a sand-covered beach, and a marina sat in the distance with boats and yachts shimmering in the sun.

Tanya's colleagues for the day were coming through the door carrying trays and bottles of wine. The floor was covered in industrial-style 'no stain' carpet, so the room could be used for many different occasions. Tanya sometimes thought of how well business was organized and how new-style functions were done in Australia compared to those in London.

London functions were surrounded by 17th century or earlier settings with old paintings to complete the atmosphere. Functions were often held in old palaces, in large rooms with massive chandeliers. People were dressed immaculately, mingling in that space like little institutions, carrying their invisible ancestral history with them wherever they went. A woman she observed earlier smiled at Tanya then extended her arm that held an empty glass. Tanya poured more wine and smiled back.

Lauren was serving, and flirting a bit, smiling with her ready-to-wear smile, and Tanya suddenly realised where Lauren's popularity was coming from. Lauren was making an effort; she was engaging herself in the conversation. Lauren was paying attention, working hard and getting results. As Lauren passed by her again, Tanya stopped her and smoothed her bow tie. Lauren smiled and then wandered around and offered a platter of canapés to another group.

Tanya noticed that Adam, one of the waiters glanced at her occasionally, but she also noticed that he talked with the same amount of zest with Lauren. Adam was taller than her, with curly black hair, pristine white shirt, black tie and friendly smile.

He was one of the myriad of people that worked for the catering agency and who came from God knew which country. There were people from all over the world that signed with the agency, earning a bit of money before they got their dream job. A job they could not find back home but somehow, miraculously thought would appear for them here in this strange land.

Tanya was not particularly interested in Adam's attention. Still, after their shift had ended, she found herself engaged in conversation with him on the way to the train station home. He was not particularly intellectual but it helped her pass the time pleasantly. Or, at least it kept her from having dark, depressive thoughts. Adam had exactly the same effect on her as any other man she happened to talk to. She could not make herself interested in men, not that they were not paying attention to her, but nobody seemed engaging enough for her to involve herself and make them special.

London, UK, 1990s

Celine was soaking in her bathtub, the hot water richly sprinkled with bath salts, but she could not get it to form thick foam. On the water's surface, there were a few lines of bubbles floating pathetically and revealing Celine's naked body. She reached for a cigarette and with the first puff almost enjoyed it until accidentally splashing it. Still she took another drag on the wet cigarette and smiled to herself. *How cunningly I had set up Maureen, that stupid cow. Now I can go to Vienna with Mark instead. Mark is such a hunk.*

The thought of him brought goose bumps to her skin, revealing fine black hair on her arms. She needed to get hair removing cream and get rid of them again. She took a deep drag on her cigarette but... nothing. She tossed it aside.

Maureen was not right for Mark, and although Maureen consistently tried to talk to him, he ignored her relentlessly. Mark had tried to ignore Celine too, but she would not be dismissed like that.

Maybe that was what prompted Celine to try even harder to talk to him, look at him; it was almost a game, and what did she have to lose? She lifted her leg above the surface of the water, admiring it in self-satisfaction. *Everything I want comes to me.* She imagined herself in a short, lime green dress, her long bare legs; pointed shoes with small but thin heels. *He will definitely not be able to resist me.*

Celine was not sure if she wanted to be with Mark, but at that moment it was all too much fun. Besides, he was her passport to staying in England. And that long look he gave her today had made her purr like a cat sitting in a sun-drenched spot.

Gina

Days were getting warmer, a real London summer. Long lines of trees in the street were heavy with green leaves that shuffled in the breeze, whispering secrets. The street was quiet; just an occasional car or bicycle passed by, breaking the silence of the midnight hour in the residential area. Gina was rushing down the street, her heart pounding. She could barely breathe. She was sure the two men sitting next to her on the bus were talking about her. That was why she got off the bus few stops earlier than she needed. Their voices still thumped in her head. They were gossiping about her.

She started running. The belt of her handbag slipped down her arm and the bag dangled, hitting against her knee. Strands of her hair fell free from the band, whipping about her face.

She could see the front door of her building, but fearing the guys were following her she ran past. *Go to Ian's place.*

She spotted a night bus across the road and ran across. Lucky there were no oncoming cars. Gina raced into the almost empty bus and hurried toward an empty seat. She did not look at the people around her, just tried to calm down. It felt good being on the lighted bus. Her head felt heavy, and her thoughts were racing. *How have I gotten myself into this situation? I did not want to be where I am now. All that rubbish in self-help books... think positive, more like be lucky.*

Gina thought positively, worked like a maniac cleaning other people's houses, and what did she get as a result? She had never felt this low, or so scared. She could not see the way forward. Just a tunnel with no light at its end. Surrounded by unfriendly people. Just no hope.

Her vision became blurred. Her chest tightened. She did not care if anybody saw her as tears rolled down her face. She was scared. She felt as if she were falling down the well deeper and deeper. Faces and people appeared in her thoughts – past mistakes, anger at being used and abused by so-called friends. *I cannot trust anybody. What if Julia tells Marco, even unintentionally, that I bought a National Insurance card for twenty pounds, and then he... or... or Julia calls the police? If they lock me up I can never return home to Bosnia again.*

Thoughts raced through her mind; she could not control them. They were erratic thoughts. Based in fear. She remembered she had not reported to the Home Office when she should have two days ago. She had meant to do it, but she had not. *What happens now?*

She stood suddenly and looked around. Two men were just behind her. Her blood thumped loudly in her head, her vision blurred, and she charged towards the doors that were just about to close.

Gina managed to get through and looked back at the guys who remained seated. They laughed diabolically at her. As she ran down the street, there was a car coming. The lights were strong and inviting. She threw herself at them. For a second she felt almost pleasure, relief – the pain and fear were gone. Just a physical and blunt hit that numbed all her senses, and left a bad metal taste in her mouth.

Melbourne, Australia, 2000s

Tanya walked home from the train station by herself. She was glad Adam did not offer to drive her. This way she knew she could keep him as a friend. He was not exactly the kind of person she would be interested in romantically. He was not the right one. Although as time went by, she was almost losing confidence that she would find the right one. Somehow everything that happened in the past seemed to be more romantic than her present.

She fell into that mood of hers where she thought she'd made a mistake moving from England to Australia. The decision to move had been made light-heartedly, always thinking she could go back to Bosnia. But that did not take into account personal change; she was a different person now. The universe shifted, and she could not go back to the point where she was before she moved away.

She had not been happy as a child. There was that constant feeling of nagging and discontent within her that she could not make better; the feeling that only with more personal wisdom, age, could she overcome these moods, these feelings. But everything she thought of in Yugoslavia seemed so dear now, everything she remembered was from another world – innocent and good, an unspoilt world.

Why had she left? Many stayed during the war and survived, lived their lives through rough times but came out of it. It was hard to call the place where one was not born, home. The memories from childhood were not here, there was nothing to remind her of that. Nobody here knew her when she was in school or had her first boyfriend. There was nobody here to judge her or tell her how much she had changed. These people that surrounded her now did not know her, they knew only this picture of her that she could distort, or make better as she wished.

She remembered times when her Macedonian-speaking neighbour would come to have coffee with her mother, and then Tanya and her friends laughing themselves silly at the mistakes the neighbour was making, mixing her Serbian and Macedonian language. That world did not exist anymore. They could talk about that for hours, laughing, and the story would stay with them forever. Even now Tanya was smiling. But that story was finished, and could never be repeated; certainly not in the same way.

Still, Tanya longed for more warmth, for a place where she could belong. But she could not imagine such a place here. Every day was almost like a pretence, and every day was yet another battle to present herself to people that did not know her. Some people around her pretended, too, but Tanya could not see them happier for it.

Tanya sometimes felt the physical pain of not being able to communicate to people, like today with Adam. There was something missing; the feeling she knew she should have once the right person came along. Still, her constant feeling of being removed from reality was not helpful. She could not concentrate on things in the present, but rather was drawn back to past happenings. She was constantly running after situations, running after happenings in her life rather than being an active part of it.

London, UK, 1990s

Celine lifted the cover off her bed and snuggled under. She felt clean and refreshed, ready to fall asleep, but not before she read a few pages of the book her best friend Helen had given her. Helen was an Oxford University graduate and the absolute *crème de la crème* of society. She'd given Celine the book after that idiot David walked out on her. The book was a set of aphorisms on feminist issues, and Celine was reading it with great pleasure, and roaring with laughter at some of the lines that accompanied the simple drawings.

Celine loved her life in London. The world was her oyster. She was thrilled to be associated at work with such important people as Helen and Robyn, the journalists at the publishing company where Celine worked. Robyn wrote articles, well articles for Good Restaurants Guide, but she was a journalist nevertheless. Celine was definitely getting on in the world. She was strong and able, and there was absolutely no obstacle she would not be able to overcome on her road to success.

Mark was a good catch. From a good English family, he held a good position within the publishing company, and oh, how he would open doors for her that she would never have been able to open herself.

The more she thought of him, the more she thought of pursuing and 'working' on getting closer to him. For a moment, she thought of Maureen, but then a sense of power overwhelmed her. Maureen just was not strong enough to do Celine any harm. Still, Celine thought that getting rid of Maureen completely would not be a bad idea. Just in case.

The most important thing was to get close to Mark; as close as possible. That was the first thing, then it was a matter of developing the right moves.

Like placing pearls on a string one by one until it became a beautiful necklace. The business trip to Vienna should secure that.

With those thoughts, she felt calm and secure, and slowly drifted off to sleep with a smile on her face.

Ian

Ian woke feeling anguished. He looked around his small bedsit; his life had not improved much since he first came to London. He was now working in a slightly better place, managing a few people in a bar, and he was earning better money – the move to this bedsit meant he could save some money.

Money was important to Ian, but it was so hard to save. The thought of Gina crossed his mind, and it sent shivers down his spine. She called him the day before from a telephone booth and said she would come to see him, but she had not appeared. He had gone around to her place around midnight, but she was not there when he checked. With Gina, there was always a problem, and although he tried to help it was to no avail – she always did as she wished. She would always turn up later, as if there were no problem at all.

Her explosive anger also felt like she was draining the life out of him. If he were honest with himself, he was losing the zest for life because of her. Her dark thoughts would put him in a bad spin that he could not shake long after she had gone.

He felt she needed those episodes as some way to vent, to get through yet another day. While he felt he was moving forward slowly, every bad day Gina had while he was around would throw him several steps back. He felt like Sisyphus pushing his stone up the mountain.

His love life was in tatters. Sure, the occasional glance or chat with somebody would appear interesting, and he went out with few girls, but it all ended on obscure terms. He was always busy meeting people but on a very superficial basis. The bar in Chelsea where he worked meant he met lots of interesting people and experienced some exciting moments, but he never thought too much of life and the direction it was taking.

Everything regarding his life felt the best he could have, considering his background. He looked at his watch and realised he had to start getting ready for work. He just hoped everything was all right with Gina.

Gina

Gina appeared at the door of the publishing company. The foyer was in dark brown colours; the floor covered in dark, sparkling clean tiles. There were a few large armchairs to one side, and a small, round table with a couple of editorial magazines on top.

The receptionist was seated behind the marble-topped desk in the corner, typing and looking into the screen. Gina approached struggling to stop the desire to just turn and run out of the building.

Instead she approached the reception desk. 'I would like to talk to Celine, please.'

'Sure, I'll call her. What is your name please?' The receptionist seemed nice in a professional, polite way.

'I... I... I... am Gina,' she managed to articulate.

'Would you happen to know Celine's extension? I seem to have a problem finding her here.'

Gina said the number surprising herself that she could recollect it. Even when she felt this hazy she always knew how to get to places, and she could recall names or numbers even when most distressed. Gina desperately wanted to talk to somebody, just to get reassured that everything would be all right.

The receptionist asked her politely to take a seat until she managed to track down Celine. Gina sat and felt as if she had not sat down all night. She could vaguely remember rushing through the dark streets of North London, as if at the end of one of them there would be salvation. What she felt was beyond scared. She was not frightened for her life; she was worried for her mind. Her feet were hurting. The end of her shirt sleeve was ripped, and it was hanging over the side of her hand, where she had a few scratches and dried blood. Her fingers were sticky with sweat and dust, but nothing mattered as much as she feared that she was losing her reasoning. The guy in the taxi that hit her was absolutely frantic when he came around to help her get up.

'Are you ok? Do you know where you're going? Do you want me to give you money for a bus?'

She'd just stood up and left him, murmuring something like: 'I am fine.'

When she turned around, he was already in the car, and leaving so fast it was as if the devil was chasing him.

Celine was not in the best of moods. Mark was out of the office, and she wanted to get him to take her out for dinner that night. She preferred to talk to him in the morning and ensure he was free for the evening. Her palms were sweaty as they always were when she felt distress.

Now her hands were shaking. *Damned Mark. Damned work. Will I ever live like all the other people do and have what I wish to have? God! Don't I deserve a break in this life? I should have worked him into asking me to out tonight, and now everything would be settled... We've got to meet tonight otherwise if I leave everything for next week it will be too late. He will forget our last encounter; the whole emotion will just fade away into obscurity. Men forget things easily. They have to be reminded many times how much they need you so they start believing it is true, that there is nothing better than what they have with you.*

Panic was rising in her. *What if he is with some other woman right now?* She could not control the situation from here. Her phone rang, and she let it ring few times hoping it would stop. But it kept annoying her to tears.

'Yes!'

'There is a girl here that wants to talk to you,' the receptionist said. 'Gina is here for you.'

'Gina... Yeah. Tell her I'll be down in ten minutes.' Celine slammed the phone down. *What else can I do now? Maybe I could take the order for breakfast for the office to the cafe, and have coffee with Gina at the same time. Mark might be back when I return.*

Celine found Gina sitting at the far corner of the foyer. As Celine approached her, she noticed Gina had a glassy expression in her eyes. 'What is the matter with you, Gina? Are you well? Look at your clothes. Have you fallen over somewhere?'

'No, I am all right.' Gina looked to the corner, as if searching for someone.

'You don't look okay Gina!' Celine led Gina out through the revolving glass door and into the suddenly-cold London summer day. 'Let's have a coffee somewhere.'

They walked into a coffee bar decorated in the French-style with a couple of pillars and some soft seats against the wall and number of round tables with two chairs on either side. As they sat next to the big glass window, it started raining outside. Busy passers-by opened their umbrellas, and others caught by the rain pulled the collars of their jackets up and ducked their heads as they hurried down the street.

'Celine, have you heard from Ian recently?'

'I spoke to him two days ago, why? Are you in some kind of trouble, Gina?' Celine stared at Gina then lit a cigarette. 'You are not pregnant, are you?' When Gina did not respond, Celine was absolutely certain that was the case. 'So you are shagging Ian, aren't you?'

Gina looked at Celine with a confused expression on her face, like she could barely understand what Celine was saying. 'No, I just wanted to see him.'

Why would you want to see him so urgently? 'You are pregnant! Go on, you can tell me!' *It can't be anything else.* Celine had a wicked look in her eyes. *God, this is exciting. Gina is pregnant!*

'I went to Ian's place yesterday, but he wasn't there.'

'Maybe, he's got someone else Gina, you can't hold him responsible for the baby.'

'What baby?'

Gina seemed very hazy. She kept turning around as if looking for somebody and then she was resting her gaze on the door of the cafe.

'I don't know Gina, I think you should abort it, get rid of it. I mean Ian is far too irresponsible to be a father.'

Gina sipped her coffee and took a drag of her cigarette. She took a long breath in and then exhaled, neither of them saying anything. Gina took a last sip from her cup and when Celine offered chewing gum she took it.

'I have to go back to work, Gina.'

'You do? Stay a bit longer... until I finish the cigarette.'

'I have to go, Gina. Do you have any money? I forgot my wallet in the office. I'll pay for the coffee next time, okay?'

Gina opened her bag then placed a five pound note on the table. They went outside into the seeping rain and loud traffic.

'Okay Gina, I have to rush. Think about getting rid of it, okay? This weekend I am going to Dublin for some research for work.' Celine stopped to check Gina's face for signs of jealousy, and then continued. 'But, call me. You know that I am too busy to call you.'

When Celine turned back, Gina was still standing there like a clueless person. Celine watched Gina from behind a bus pole, checking the woman's movements. A few moments later Gina returned to the café. *She is weird. Too much time on her hands, I say.* Celine snuggled into her mohair jacket, pulling her hands into the sleeves and hurried towards the sandwich bar. *I have far too many problems of my own to worry about Gina and her silly, disorganised life.*

CHAPTER II

London, UK, 1990s

Ian was walking home from work, and as he entered the tube station he heard the train pulling up to platform. In his rush Ian bumped into a rugged-looking guy at the ticket machine slot. Ian apologised, but it seemed that was not enough as the guy shouted a few nasty words while punching the air. Ian apologised again then ran down the moving escalator, but the train was on its slow move away. *Blast. Next tube is not coming for another fifteen minutes. Miserable Northern line!*

As he sat on the bench, Ian noticed the rough-looking guy from the barriers and the guy noticed him too. The man stood there for a little while as if in thought but then turned and walked to the other side. Ian breathed a sigh of relief. He did not need that kind of trouble, not with the kind of visa he had. He again felt like a miserable immigrant, unable to even defend himself. Still, it would have been unbearable and far more miserable were he back home in some trench, covered with mud and suffering in the cold. Going forward was the only way, and London was the right place to do so.

Ian was looking forward to tonight's party. There should be quite a few Yugoslavs there, and he liked the idea of being part of that, of belonging somewhere. It always made him feel better when he was surrounded by people he knew shared similar problems and worries. His good friend Igor, who was also from Sarajevo, had managed to leave just before the war. Ian had not been so lucky and was caught and held prisoner along with his parents. The whole episode was ghastly, and often plagued his sleep; waking from a nightmare in the middle of the night thinking he was still in prison. His parents moved to Banja Luka the same time Ian moved to London.

His grandparents lived in Banja Luka, and Ian spent many happy school holidays with his grandparents.

Neither he nor his parents thought much of the problems when troubles started brewing and slowly unfolding in Bosnia, they just thought life had become a bit rough. Unemployment started rising as companies collapsed, and those who still had jobs were even less secure than they were the decade before. Ian and his family ignored the first signs of neighbours retreating into their own flats, not venturing out much. Some neighbours started moving to Croatia and Serbia, but even that did not alarm Ian and his family. Muslims were mainly remaining, and they appeared to be attending mosques more. Ian and his family even celebrated the New Year, the last one in peace, with their neighbour Kemal.

In their block of flats, there was one Croat, Josip. He was a retired clerk who earned his pension working in Zagreb. Josip left his adult children in Zagreb when he returned to Sarajevo – he loved the place he was born, and could not live without it anymore. Josip was also at the New Year's party that had started rather solemnly, but somehow an argument soon began on whether Tito should have allowed the 1974 referendum. Ian and his brother had glanced at each other with a puzzled expression. Noticing this Kemal had explained:

'With that referendum Tito gave the right to each Republic or province to separate from the rest of Yugoslavia and eventually secede.'

'Let them separate if they want to.' Ian shrugged.

'It wasn't Tito who gave the right, it was decided by the people.' Josip was defensive, and they all looked at Josip, concerned.

'Tito was looking after you Croats, wasn't he? We stupid Serbs just did what we were told,' Ian's father said.

'Tito could have been Serb for all I know.' Josip fumed as he pulled out a cigarette then threw the box back on the table.

'Of course, you are right, Josip.' Kemal was the only one composed after this unexpected outburst.

Ian pulled his mother's sleeve, beckoning with his head to the door. Ian, his brother and parents left soon after. His parents went to bed while Ian and his brother stayed up and complained about yet another flimsy New Year Eve's TV program. Ian noticed that Kemal's wife was less friendly than usual and this was discussed the following morning at breakfast. In the next few months the war in Croatia started and with this, things changed irrevocably in the neighbourhood.

The train finally pulled into the station and Ian found a seat and took out his book. Written by an English writer, Ian used such books to try and immerse himself into the society that now surrounded him, trying to understand the culture and enjoy it as much as possible. He often wondered at his chances of staying in the country. His lawyer was very positive about his chances, but the feeling of uncertainty was daunting. It was not easy to get used to this new style of living, especially coming from a country where neighbours knew what was being prepared in someone's house for lunch, to now where you did not even know your neighbours at all.

Sometimes he thought returning to what was Yugoslavia might not be such a tragedy. But, this thought was rare. His brother had returned, but now wanted to come back to England. There was no sign of improvement in Serbia. Ian knew his options were very limited, that if he were to have any semblance of life he had to invent it here.

There was a hint of a relationship in his life, but it was rather vague. He was seeing an English girl, Carol, although it was very sporadic dating. If he called, she would often have other plans, while whenever she called him, they would usually meet.

He had known Carol for about three months, knew very little about her and had not met any of her family – but she was not close to them. Their conversations were forced and they often had long spells of uncomfortable silence, he even sensed that she was seeing someone else, and that she kept Ian just in case the other option failed. He did not mind. After all, there was not much to lose, and he preferred to spend his time with someone rather than sit at home alone.

The train pulled into the station and he made his way outside. As he stepped onto the pavement he zipped up his leather jacket and hurried toward his flat. He spotted a woman who looked very much like Gina running towards the bus then disappearing into it.

Sarajevo, Bosnia, 1990s

Electricity was out yet again. Twenty-four hours they had said on the radio, but thirty-six hours later Momir and his mother were still in a cold, dark flat. *Thirty-two years of age and still living with my mother, waiting for her to go out and buy me cigarettes.*

Their neighbours were new and did not visit at all, his mother did not know them other than to say hello when she met them on the stairs. His mother was always worried over him hiding at home; she did not like to live with the risk of having someone calling the military police to check why he was not conscripted for the Bosnian army.

Some neighbours had lost brothers, sisters, parents, close relatives, and there was mistrust in abundance – anger and bitter feelings ripe amongst the refugees themselves but also the locals.

Momir lit the last cigarette from the packet. Peace and quiet. He watched the street through the thin curtain; the building opposite was also dark, the moon sitting just above it. He thought of times when he was watching this same moon with his friends years ago, as they sat in cafés and sipped bottles of beer for hours and discussing how soon it would be before the first tourist visited the moon. It felt so close then and it felt so far away now. Momir remembered how he argued with Ian, who did not believe that life only existed on Earth:

'I mean, why should the Earth only have good conditions for living? In this vast universe there has to be another planet where the conditions are as good for some form of life. I am not saying there are people just like us, but then again, that would depend on the type of conditions, and that the first signs of life then had to develop and evolve.'

Ian lived in London now; his parents now lived in the heavily-Serbian side of Bosnia. Momir pulled a last drag from the cigarette, the taste of the filter still bitter in his mouth. Momir had only received one letter from Ian, he was okay, working in a restaurant... and asked Momir to leave Bosnia.

Momir had lain awake many nights thinking of that prospect. Many of his friends had left Bosnia, why couldn't he? *Am I a coward? Am I scared to leave even the poor comfort of the apartment for something completely unknown but definitely better?*

To leave this city where every corner was so familiar, to abandon this city where he could run blindfolded from one end to the other without bumping into as much as an overgrown hedge. His mother had stopped asking him to find a better life for himself, and this did not help his feelings of inadequacy. So he remained in Bosnia, hiding in their apartment and hoping to survive the next day, living like an animal in a cave while his mother was bringing home food and the occasional pack of cigarettes.

Life was happening but he was not part of it.

The key tuned in the lock and the front door opened, his mother's heavy breathing after climbing the stairs drifted around their apartment. He could hear her putting a few contents on the kitchen table, then the fridge opening as she deposited a few pieces there. Then the bread box opened and closed.

He dozed. There was not much more to do. When he woke he sat straighter; there was a small coffee table in front of him and framed needle point work his aunt did years ago on the wall. A credenza held small porcelain figurines and a set of coffee cups and saucers for "special occasions".

His mother walked into the room. 'Why are you sitting in the dark? Why don't you light a candle?'

'What for? I'm not doing anything. We need candles. Save them,' he said.

Mother left then returned with a half-burnt candle sitting in a glass ashtray. Candlelight lit her face as she settled in the small armchair placing the candle on the coffee table. She remained silent.

Sometimes Momir would watch his neighbours through the spy hole. Most of them he did not know. Some of his neighbours came from the smaller villages that surrounded Sarajevo, taking the opportunity to occupy apartments vacated by those who had fled. Some of his pre-war neighbours had left everything behind. Some had to leave; others were taken into war-created prisons that were often called concentration camps.

Momir would see those new neighbours through thin curtains as they moved quickly down the street, gazes straining towards the mountains surrounding the city.

Sometimes he would see these same neighbours late at night, in a full uniform, bent under the weight of uncertain nights at the front. They walked like men much older than their age.

Momir felt guilty when he saw them; he should be at the front alongside them. He was glad he did not have to face them. He moved away from the window, certain that they did not want to talk about their experiences. They were only cogs in much bigger machinery. Momir was certain of that.

He knew that he would not be spared from conscription if he was found at the apartment. Momir was able bodied despite his diagnosis of mental instability.

At the very beginning of the war he had been conscripted into the Yugoslav army, and the experience still haunted him. He did not feel comfortable talking or meeting with active soldiers, and felt much removed from the whole idea of Serbian kingdom and national pride. *Why were the Serbs accused of fostering the idea of creating Greater Serbia?* This was all very alien to him. By now he felt removed from his old Muslim and Croat neighbours. All he felt now was isolation.

Often at night the sight of a burning old man would appear before him. The old man's body convulsed as his skin tightened, blistered, charred. He would look Momir in the eyes, but it was not pain Momir saw in the old man's eyes, just acceptance. The smell of burning flesh was overpowering, and Momir would wake with this scent stinging in his nostrils.

Waking from the nightmare offered no relief, just a deep sense of purposelessness. The eyes of the old man peered from beyond the grave. Momir would spend hours awake, night after night until dawn broke into the room. *What am I doing here?* But he also knew that those eyes would follow him anywhere he went, and the smell would always linger, like a devil whose mission it was to ensure he never saw a happy day again. *There is no better life anywhere else. I had left it behind years ago.*

When he was first conscripted it did not feel serious. There were some troubles, he was aware of divisions between Muslims, Croats and Serbs, but it all seemed to be the same old story. He was convinced it would all die down and everything would go back to normal. Even when he donned the uniform and went to live in army barracks in early 1991, he was positive about a good and peaceful outcome. Muslims and Croats were leaving the army, escaping overnight, there was confusion in the JNA army, mostly Serbs were left and then fighting became Serbs against the other nations rather than a general fight for peace and preservation of Yugoslavia.

He followed orders but knew those orders were coming from the higher-ups in the army, who were thrown into this mayhem as much as the ground soldiers. Times were confusing. Some of his friends had already left the country. In the midst of all of that, he was still hoping. The town was in mayhem, buses with people were leaving.

Only when he was moved to the outskirts of Sarajevo and into the surrounding mountains where another army waited, did he realise that he had unknowingly taken a side.

He was sleeping with others in barns, abandoned houses, mud-filled trenches... They were attacking villages. Younger people in the villages had left already;

only the older folk remained. Some villages were Serbian, some Muslim, some mixed. There were few Croatians in the mixed villages. All of a sudden he became aware of nationality – this had never been important before. It was cold, his socks were often wet and hard from dirt, his rifle stuck to his fingers, and there was smell of gunpowder in the air every day.

One day a group of them went to a village that seemed abandoned. All of a sudden an explosion ripped through the air. He was followed closely by Dragan.

They both turned and ran back to their fellow soldiers. Misa was lying in a pool of blood, a river of red gushing from the stump of his right arm. The right leg of his trousers was in tatters, with open wounds below his knee-cap and on his thigh. He was sprawled across the front staircase of the house as if he was a rag doll. The door was smashed into pieces and the scene covered in black dust, the gunpowder smell pinching their nostrils.

Tears rolled down Momir's face before he heard, 'Come, quick, get his legs, I'll grab him by the arms.'

Sasa threw his rifle to his back and stood above Misa's head, bending down to grab his back. Momir came closer to Misa, put his hand across his mouth and then removed it looking into Misa's vacant eyes.

'There is no point,' Momir said, looking at Sasa. 'He's gone.'

'I'm not leaving him here.' Sasa looked at others.

'We'll have to for the moment, we'll come back when night falls.'

Commander Sveto appeared at the scene. He approached Miso's lifeless body, took his hand and put his thumb on Misa's wrist then shook his head.

Momir and the others returned to the barn late that evening, they didn't talk to the others; each was lost in their own world. The commander left by jeep, lights turned off.

'Did he have brothers or sisters?' Dragan asked.

'No, he was an only child,' Sasa said.

London, UK, 1990s

Celine returned to her office feeling smug and elated, and found Maureen sitting in her office.

'I saw you leaving with that friend of yours. Girl from your country?'

'Yes, we went for a coffee. You seem to see a lot.'

'You think so? I also noticed that Mark is getting married.'

Celine paled and turned her back to Maureen. 'You mean Mark from our office?' Her heart was pounding, and she sat trying to compose herself.

'Yes. Our Mark. His girlfriend is pregnant.'

'I didn't know he had a girlfriend.'

'Neither did he!' Maureen was in fits of laughter.

Celine tried to fake laugh too, but she knew it sounded pathetic.

Maureen was a good-looking girl in her late-twenties with long, dark-brown hair. Celine knew Maureen was interested in Mark but they never discussed that nor had

Mark mentioned it. Maureen was Celine's biggest threat when it came to Mark.

Interrupted by the arrival of their boss, Celine was glad to be rid of Maureen, but when left on her own, Celine felt a nauseating sense of desperation. Mark was her perfect opportunity to secure a passport. *He just cannot marry some bimbo!* Warm tears started welling in her eyes. *Bad, bloody luck. That was all that her life was about. Just constant hurdle after hurdle!* She was petrified of having to go back to Kosovo, the terrible low life that was lived there – she could not take it. Not anymore. Her neighbours were nosy, looking into each other lives, there was no privacy.

Everybody knew what the other had for dinner. *Please God don't let that happen.* And she could not even begin to imagine the sense of failure when neighbours saw her return from London. She would be the talk of the town. *God! Don't let me sink that low.* But then, a small ray of hope snuck in through a crack in her dark thoughts: *What if none of this is true?* Celine tried to recall the look in Maureen's eyes. *Was she, maybe, just saying that to check my reaction?*

Mark

Mark pushed the button for the lift, checking his reflection in the shiny polished door and straightened his dark-blue jacket. His white shirt was crisp, and the blue tie matched perfectly. He ran fingers through his blond hair then stroked his chin, checking it was well shaved. This morning's meeting went well and he felt good about himself. There was only one other serious competitor, and if Mark had made a better offer, Clarke Press Publishing would get the project. First, though, he had to get to his desk and read his email in case there were some messages from the editor, then it was off to tell the boss about the meeting.

As he passed by the bay where Celine worked, she struck up a conversation, and she did not appear to be feeling well. 'Have you had some bad news from home?' he asked.

'No,' she said, 'they are all okay. How are you?'

He still was not assured; she just did not look all right, not her normal self. But if she said she was okay... 'We must have dinner together soon,' he said and tried to leave it at that.

Celine smiled. 'Yes, when shall we do that?'

'What about this Friday?' Mark responded quickly.

'Yes, that's good.' Celine feigned a lack of enthusiasm, although it was excitement she was feeling.

'We'll meet at the restaurant, the one I know of in Chelsea? I'll book the table.'

'Yes, that's fine.' *The first puzzle piece is in place,* Celine thought.

Mark rearranged a few papers on his desk as he waited for his computer to boot up. He opened his emails.

A message from Kate. He didn't feel like reading it. The news she'd delivered a couple of days earlier had been hard to cope with. He liked her, but when she'd told him about her pregnancy, he'd felt like he was being choked. He hadn't known how to react, so he'd just smiled and hugged her avoiding giving any definitive answers until the news settled in.

He'd managed to kiss her, feeling too confused for any true display of emotion. He'd tried to remain strong as thoughts raced through his mind, but had been relieved when she'd left soon after so he could reflect in peace and confront the fact that she was pregnant. He had feelings for her, but was that enough to marry her? She was pretty, rather petite, and with beautiful straw-blond hair and green eyes. But was she the love of his life?

He immediately thought of Melanie, the girl he'd met at a pub in the country. After only few exchanged sentences he'd felt as if they'd known each other forever. She'd invited him to her home the next day and he'd been greatly surprised when he'd arrived and found a wide drive leading to the entrance of the house between the large bodies of trees.

He'd had to double-check the house number in case he'd made a mistake, but he'd been at the right place. The gates opened automatically and he drove through to the castle-like house at the end of driveway. A sense of old and established family enveloped him as he looked at the light brown walls and steps that led to the large dark brown door.

Melanie was already walking down the stairs as he exited the car. She'd kissed him on the cheek and led him inside to what could only have been a library. The walls were covered with row upon row of books, and when she'd gone he'd slowly browsed through: history, philosophy, biographies, art... An older gentle-looking man in a tweed suit had entered the room, and Mark had been unsure as to how to greet him.

The man made it easy as he approached Mark and shook his hand. 'Hello I'm George. Melanie's father.'

'Mark. Nice to meet you... sir.'

George had engaged him in a delightfully light conversation and Mark was pleased to be able to sit and chat with him. Melanie had returned with coffee and only managed to enrich the conversation. He'd felt comfortable with them, relaxed and wherever his eyes rested there was a nice piece of antique furniture, comfortable yet classy.

'Melanie told me you work for a publishing company? You must be enjoying such an interesting environment.'

'Yes, I'm trying to venture more into enlarging the business but at the moment my main work is with young writers trying to publish their first book. At times, it's how shall I put it, disenchanting, as not all of them get published. In some cases, I can help them get their work into a more publishable standard but it's not always possible. Occasionally, I'll come across a real gems, that with little editing, become so hot we cannot wait to have it published. The others, well... I try to be sympathetic and give them the bad news in a pleasant and gentle way.'

Mark sipped his coffee and relaxed into the armchair. A short pause ensued. Mark rested letting the other two take it in.

'What sort of work were you involved in?' Mark asked, taking another sip.

George seemed to be ready to reply, but Melanie took over. 'Father used to work in the oil industry. He's a chemical engineer.'

'Have you travelled a lot due to your work?' Mark was genuinely interested.

'I have, as a matter of fact. By the time I was in my fifties I held more senior positions so....'

'Father was one of the executive members of the Board that governed the company.'

'Right... I was with the company for over thirty years and, as a result, one gets to do more senior jobs. I got to travel a lot, not only to the US but the Far East, South Asia, Russia, South America. But, those were different times, in the seventies when oil was vast or at least ...' Mark was listening to George but occasionally glanced at Melanie. For a moment he thought that she looked at him and then at her father with the same expression of pride in her eyes. '...I feel it's my duty.'

Mark knew that he'd have to leave soon, a visit too long would be inappropriate, but he was sure he would be back here.

He'd never returned. He'd gone back to London and work had taken up all of his time. A week after meeting Melanie he'd met Kate in London. One thing led to another, and their relationship became, or appeared to be, more solid. He'd learned Melanie had gone travelling, and he still hoped they would meet again. They never did.

Mark emailed Kate, trying to sound relaxed, trying to cover the uncertainty he felt about their life together. A life, he believed, now seemed totally inevitable.

Sarajevo, Bosnia, 1990s

Kemal woke early that morning. He hoped the war would end soon and that his son and grandson would be home before Ramadan. But then, he was also aware that, with this war, they would finally get their country; and for that, it was worth waiting and spending many sleepless nights glued to the radio listening to troop advances for his son and grandson's unit. Kemal got up, washed his hands, then with his rosary beads, slowly began to pray.

His thoughts were with the brave fighters, and his prayers for the final liberation. He thought of Bosnia in its former glory with Aga[1] titled men and good old families keeping together. He thought of times when they would have been in the mosque and enjoying their chat after prayer, kids playing around, their innocence guarded and preserved. Every time a mosque got blown up, it was like a dagger to his heart. He would not eat for days, and his beads would get hot from his fingers pressing against them, rolling it on its thread from one side to the other. He knew their leaders would fulfil their promise in building a bigger and better mosque in its place.

A knock to the door brought him back to reality.

'Selam, Father. Did you sleep well?'

'Merhaba[2], Selma. I slept better than your husband and your son, that is for certain.'

---

1   Aga - member of aristocracy, title earned by military achievement in Ottoman Empire occupied countries
2   Merhaba - greeting, turkish

'Do you want your coffee and Turkish Delight now or after breakfast? We only have two pieces of the sweet left.'

'Bring me my coffee, my petal,' he said. 'Soon we will have our sweets. We will have much more than that. Everything we once had we'll have back again if Allah wants. And, Allah is great and loving, and he gives to the good and righteous. We will have everything just like in the old times. Beautiful women, like yourself Selma, will be walking down the street in their pretty shalvare[3] and sandals, so you can hear them walking down the wooden staircase like a beautiful song. Smelling of jasmine and laughing from happiness and a good cheerful life. And our young men looking at them; handsome and brave in white shirts, white like snow on the mountain and waistcoats red like blood. Their trousers green like the serge in the mosque, green like the grass in our valleys where sheep graze and a shepherd stands nearby happy to live their life. Not like now. But, times will be better Selma, believe me.'

Selma was gazing at Kemal. A light smile brushed over her lips. Her father-in-law's stories always filled her with calm, and she felt assured that whatever happened would be for the best. She knew Kemal believed that if Allah decided to take her husband and son away that, too, would be for the best.

'Go, Selma. Bring me the coffee and let me pray for the better life, for the beauty to return to our streets and for smiles to return to our children's faces.'

When left alone, Kemal returned to his dream of their town being the way it was when he was a small boy. Main

---

3   shalvare - female, usually Muslim women, traditional loose trousers

street covered with cobblestone and lined with small shops and coffee houses where elders were drinking their hot coffees and watching passers-by. Noise was coming from many shops as young men shaped copper plates into dishes, wove baskets, repaired shoes; the sweet smell of freshly-baked pie drifted from bakeries and people passed through happily.

As Muslim cleric Hodza[4] passed down the street, people would stop what they were doing to greet him. The unfortunate ones would bow down, and kiss his hand asking for a prayer for their ill ones, or thanking him for something he did for them or their family.

Selma walked back into the room quietly. She put the coffee down and left the room as she heard somebody ringing the bell at the front door.

London, UK, 1990s

Ian was sitting in his room feeling distressed. He'd seen Gina the day before and having just returned from her place he felt even more disturbed by the way she had behaved and spoken. Gina was so very different from the people he met. She had this enormous capacity for suffering, and he sometimes thought she was doing it in order to get him to do things for her. He felt completely sapped of energy; nobody else lived the way she did. Gina was from the old neighbourhood, and he felt a sense

---

4   Hodza - Muslim cleric, head of the mosque, and very prominent figure in town, very well educated in Islamic studies

of responsibility for her. Their parents were very close friends, and they grew up together until Ian's family moved to Sarajevo.

Every time Gina knocked on the door his heart skipped a beat as he would worry that some calamity had befallen her again. She could not hold even cleaning jobs for longer than a few weeks. She would always leave her jobs angry, and would blame others for the reasons she left, going on to describe them in the most awful way.

It was a terrible insight. Could he be one of those awful people? Gina's behaviour hurt him and he would often light a candle for her when in church. She was saying some crazy things when he had seen her earlier, and he could not believe they were true. She was suffering deeply, and he wondered if he was actually helping her. Did he care enough for her? He tried to keep himself sane, strived for a normal life but he always felt different from those "normal" people he met. And after being with Gina he always felt less worthy.

Gina covered him with a dark energy he could not shake for days, and she would leave him believing the world was a bad place, and where decent people were few and far between.

Celine

Celine was getting ready for her work. *Dinner with Mark tonight.* She studied her reflection in the mirror. *How could Mark not see how attractive I am?* But the thought of another girl possibly being pregnant to Mark made her furious, but a deep misery soon took over. *Those small-time girls, wasting no time, jumping at anything to acquire married status. Disgusting.* She had worked too hard to get close to Mark to give up just like that. She needed to think of a way for Mark to get out of that situation and keep him for herself, then everything would be okay.

She would do her utmost to make Mark crazy about her. There was no way she could face going back to Kosovo, to where her neighbours would absolutely revel in her misfortune. Feeling rather down and seriously doubting the possibility of having Mark to herself she applied her lipstick, checked herself in the mirror then took her bag and walked out the door.

Sarajevo, Bosnia, 1990s

Momir woke to another cold January morning. He could hear his mother pottering around in the kitchen – she always had something to do around the house. He knew he should go to the basement and get a few pieces of wood for the stove, but he also knew that he could not leave the apartment. He had to rely on his mother for everything. Watching her do so much work made him feel useless; his life seemed so worthless. He could not go to war. He just could not hold a gun in his hands anymore. It would seem in contrast to all he believed in, to do such a thing. To aim at somebody, shoot at somebody, run and hide around shelled houses and throw grenades in order to clear the way. No, he could not do that. He might be forcibly removed from his room one day by the soldiers of the newly-formed country – whatever that country might be – and he might be paraded on the streets as a coward. How small a human life was when faced with the prospect of war.

This stupid siege was so out of control. The idiots occupying the city were not following reason but blindly following commands.

Hiding behind the thin curtains of his room, he had seen countless figures running across the street and looking nervously toward the high mountains surrounding the city. He knew that on top of those mountains, the ones shooting were probably some of his mates, guys he went to school with. Had it ever crossed their minds that they might aim and shoot at one of their own?

Melbourne, Australia, 2000s

As she was preparing to go out, Tanya realised she was not really interested in attending the party. She had not expected to be invited, but she had, and she finally decided it was a better option than staying home. Her hair would not sit in the place; it kept maintaining its own independence. *Maybe I should just stay in. Nobody will miss me.*

But then a stronger urge made her reconsider. It was unfair to the people who had invited her. *I'll go and just leave early.* It did not feel like a good way to spend an evening, talking to people she did not know. At her age, she should be doing different things, but the possibilities of meeting someone were much more frequent when she was younger, now those possibilities were scarce at best. The ones she did meet were much less reliable. Pressure from her family overseas was also on the wane. Obviously they'd given up. Tanya was not sure if that was something to be pleased about, or panicked by – that she was past the age where she should have settled down, or even those closest to her weren't bothered to keep reminding her anymore.

Do I actually care what people think? Even if I do care, there is very little I could change. How do I appear to others? An unmarried maid.

The thoughts welling up in her head did not do much to put her in good spirits for the party. Nevertheless, she did the best she could with her hair, dabbed a bit more loose powder on her face to cover up the imperfections brought on by aging, but that also made her face appear more fresh. She was never a beauty. She put on her coat and left the house.

As Tanya walked into the party, it was beginning to pick up. A few more people arrived the same time she did, more following soon after. One of the guys started talking to her, and while he told her his name, she soon forgot it. He was talking into her ear as she was scanning the crowd. A blond guy kept looking at her from across the room. His blue eyes were so piercing, but it was hard for Tanya to decide if it was his intense personality that was so piercing or just the colour of his eyes.

Tanya glanced at him couple of times, but then he got talking to a pleasant-looking man of about her age. He had an air of a 'fulfilled' man, casually but neatly dressed in a crisp white shirt and clean jeans, so she guessed that he was married. This made her feel even more comfortable when the two men walked and stood next to her that she relaxed into conversation with the married man knowing that there would be no emotional situations with him.

Soon after, the married man Steve, offered her to sit down with him and his friend Malcolm – blue-eyed guy. Tanya started talking to Malcolm, and he was engaging her in conversation very intensely. She found it very easy to discuss things with him as he was responding eagerly. As the night wore on; she found herself alone with Malcolm. They were quite wrapped in a conversation, and she enjoyed it, but it was time to leave, so she stood, pleased to have spent an interesting evening.

Malcolm rose too and seemingly unsure, offered to see her again.

'Yes, sure,' Tanya said and gave him her number. As he pulled her towards him she turned her head and he kissed her cheek.

She went home, and for the first time in a long time, slept well. Somehow, things felt right, and her life seemed to be turning in the right direction.

Sarajevo, Bosnia, 1990s

In the middle of the night the phone rang. Once, twice, then on the third ring Selma finally reached it and picked up the receiver...

'Yes, I am his wife. No, his father is asleep. Can't you tell me? Was he hurt? Right, I'll get his father.'

Selma went to Kemal's room where he was already sitting upright in his bed.

'It is for you, Father.'

'Don't worry my dear, everything will be all right,' Kemal told her. Kemal walked to the phone determined but not rushing. 'Kemal speaking. Right. I see. No, we will not panic. I understand. May Allah be with you. Any news about them is good news.'

Kemal put the phone down and patted Selma on the shoulder then walked into the lounge and seated his sizeable body onto a large ottoman. He put his legs up and brought them closer to his body. He breathed a sigh of a heavy heart.

'What happened, Father?' Selma knelt on the seat next to the ottoman. 'Has something happened to them? Have they been hurt?'

Kemal looked into her frightened face. 'No. Their unit has been cut off. There was some intense fighting with the Serbian army and the unit where our boys are, were left behind. According to their commander they have not been captured. We will pray they will be back alive and well.'

Selma grabbed her head, stood, turned around in despair. She cried aloud, 'God, where are you? Where are they? Help them!' She banged her fists against her forehead and stared at Kemal. 'Oh, my! How can you appear so peaceful when I know that you suffer?' she cried in disbelief.

'Selma, sit down here. What will be, will be. By crying and carrying on, you are not helping anybody. We need all our strength to help them.'

Selma sat, seemingly sapped of her energy, and a state of stupor grew on her face.

They sat in silence for a while. Only Kemal's hard breathing could be heard. Then Kemal took his beads, and began rolling them on the thread, praying quietly with only the sound of night crickets breaking the rarely quiet hour of the night in the besieged Sarajevo. Kemal looked at Selma lost in her thoughts and two streams of tears rolled down her fearful face. He put his hand on her shoulder, but she did not respond.

Melbourne, Australia, 2000s

...Tanya did not know the man sitting next to her, but moments later he stood, a look of disgust on his face as he left. She could not recall what it was she had done wrong, and she tried to call out at him, but her words refused to come...

Tanya woke with a start, concentrating on her dream but feeling blank. She felt the dream was connected to Malcolm and that any kind of relationship was doomed to fail before it began.

She felt so despondent that she did not feel like getting up at all. Then her thoughts turned to Gina and Ian. Tears welled in her eyes; she was overwhelmed by a sense of guilt and misery that she should be doing better.

She should not have been in this situation at this stage of her life. All the wasted opportunities and wasted moments of her life were gone forever, her life in a new land where connections were so fragile, where her feeling of belonging was like broken threads. *Maybe my dream did not have any connection to Malcolm. Why has he not called? He will call, though, I feel it.* The idea of a possible romance made her feel more optimistic.

A relationship will fix all that was and is wrong. It will heal all the lost opportunities, and everything will be fine again.

It did not exactly make her feel better, but for a moment it patched up some of the ragged emotions that bred inside her day and night. She hardly heard from Gina anymore, and Ian only sent her emails every now and then. He seemed confused but struggling for the better. She called her mother often, as a dutiful daughter does, but sometimes the connection could not be made. When she did talk to her mother, she was comforted by the woman's level-headed approach to everything.

Tanya rarely thought of her friends from childhood or teenage years, as it made her feel uncomfortable, uneasy to recall those times. She often felt her life was like a card game, and she had always been dealt a bad hand.

London, UK, 1990s

Celine travelled on the tube, unable to contain her excitement. She and Mark were going to have dinner and discuss the trip to Vienna. *I am going to be successful. My dreams will come true.*

For a moment, a thought of suspicion crossed her mind: what if Mark was going to have a baby with Kate. She would find out tonight. Some nasty little gold digger was not going to take her place.

Celine got to the restaurant, and glanced inside to see if Mark had arrived. He was sitting at a table near the window and was busy looking through the menu. He did not notice her.

A waiter ushered her to the table and Mark smiled warmly, stood, extended his hand in a warm handshake and pulled the chair out for her. 'How are you?' Mark asked.

'Have you been waiting for long?'

'Not at all.'

'It's a lovely restaurant,' said Celine as she looked around.

'They have great food,' said Mark with a smile.

'So the trip to Vienna is on the cards?' Celine decided it was best to get straight to the point, and quickly. Mark looked at her, confused. 'I mean, finally we will get the possibility to extend overseas,' Celine continued, 'and Vienna is the place to be.' She pulled back a bit after that remark, giving the conversation over to Mark.

'Well, yes, that is one way of looking at it,' he said.

'Was it your idea to venture in that direction?' Celine bumped his ego a bit more.

'Well, yes and no. As you said, it's important to show our presence there and try and get into the market where a different language—'

'So, I guess you might need my German-language skills. My father used to work in Vienna. He is retired now.'

'Was he in the publishing business also?'

Celine felt uncomfortable. 'No, he was in the building industry. They built many buildings around Vienna. I don't understand much of that.' She smiled flirtatiously.

'How interesting. So you would feel comfortable going to Vienna? I presume you've visited.'

Celine nodded. 'I would feel very comfortable in Vienna and I have confidence in you.' She looked into his eyes and smiled ever so lightly. He looked at her with directness, and smiled with a manly confidence before taking a sip of water. She knew that now was the right moment to act.

She extended her arm across the table and touched his hand with hers, pretending to be reaching for flowers in a small vase decorating the table. 'You do know that I enjoy being with you,' she said, and the expression on his face darkened. 'I mean you are very competent at your job, and I could learn a lot.' A smile lightened his features. 'I like your face when you smile.' This was followed by another flirtatious smile from Celine.

'Thank you, hmm. Shall we order?' Mark blurted nervously.

'Yes, of course,' said Celine taking a menu and looking through it. She put the menu aside. 'I have already started the presentation, and thought you might want to see it. Possibly correct it?'

Mark smiled. 'That's a good suggestion. Very good.'

I wish I could reach across the table and kiss him.

As the dinner date was coming to a close, Celine felt comfortable. They were laughing, getting closer, and he did not at all act threatened by her, but rather accepting of her charms. As they stood, he made way for her to walk to the door first, and then he opened it for her.

Celine turned to Mark. 'I really enjoyed this evening, Mark. Let's do it again some time.'

'I had an excellent time, too.' Mark offered a wide smile.

'I hope you won't be doing any work tonight.'

'As a matter of fact I will. There are some reports I need to complete.'

Time to act. Again.

'Does your girlfriend help with it, is she still... are you still together?' There was a cloud lingering over his face. 'I mean I don't want to intrude.' Celine looked intently into his face.

'Things are bit hard there at the moment,' he said, 'I'd rather not talk about it.'

Celine leaned towards him. 'I've had a wonderful evening. Thanks ever so much.' Celine wrapped her arms around his shoulders, her breasts pressed against his chest as she gave him an innocent peck on the cheek. 'I'll see you Monday.' She looked at him, pulled the sides of her light coat to reveal her figure. Mark reacted by lowering his gaze towards her legs, and she added with a smile, 'I can't wait.'

Melbourne, Australia, 2000s

Tanya still felt confident Malcolm would call despite three weeks passing since he had taken her phone number. She had started a new job at a travel agency; it was only part-time and temporary, but she hoped they might keep her on long term. The agency was close to where she lived, and the company was impressed with her being able to speak a couple of languages. And as she was from Europe, this also meant she could give more personal advice with regard to travelling to certain countries. Her job was still very basic – answering phones and booking flights here and there.

That morning Tanya was working the early shift and had waited five minutes before her boss, Maggie, arrived.

'Morning!' Maggie was as pleasant as ever. 'Have you waited long?' she asked, and before Tanya could reply added: 'I had to take Charlotte to school, my husband couldn't. Anyway, here I am.'

She turned to Tanya with a smile letting her through the door first. 'I'll be staying for twenty minutes, checking emails, then I'll have to go to a meeting. I should be back just before you leave. I hope that's okay with you.'

Again, without waiting for the answer Maggie walked into her office and closed the door. Tanya sat at her desk, turned on the computer and started to organise the work that had been left on her desk. She barely noticed Maggie's farewell as her boss left.

While Maggie was out, Tanya had a few enquiries, but nobody bought a ticket, although some left their numbers.

A younger looking man walked in mid-morning and Tanya immediately had the feeling she knew him, a feeling that often occurred when she happened to meet someone from her old country. 'Good morning. Can I help you?'

'I was looking for a trip to London. Would you have anything?'

His accent was strong and as he continued it was more obvious that he was from her old country, so she felt quite comfortable asking, 'Do you speak Serbo-Croatian?'

'I speak Macedonian,' he said. 'As a matter of fact, as soon as I saw your name badge, I knew we wouldn't have to speak English. My name's Goran.'

Tanya nodded. 'So, you want to fly to London?'

'Well, yes and no. I don't like it here very much, so I was wondering if I should maybe try it in London. It's closer to Macedonia, and I might be able to go and see my parents more often.'

There was an air of sympathy around him. His stare was like being captured in a fine spider's web. The longer she sat there the more intricate the web became. She felt quite caught in it; melting in that web and bewitched by his Mediterranean good looks. Goran was very nonchalant when he finally said: 'Give me your number and I'll call you some time and we'll meet for a coffee. How's that?'

Tanya gave him her number still in a trance from this intense yet almost familiar experience. When Goran left she felt vulnerable and light as a feather and quite defenceless. There were now two guys with her telephone number in their pockets wandering somewhere around Melbourne.

London, UK, 1990s

Mark found a seat closer to the back of the bus, and as he sat, his thoughts returned to Kate. He would have to see her soon. His chest tightened at the thought. Is this the end of the road? Had he been pushed against the wall without any options? *I'm being too cruel. Kate is a good woman. She loves me, and I'll learn to love her. Especially when the child comes.* He extended his arm and opened a small butterfly window. A dash of fresh air calmed him. *I'll marry her. It's the right thing to do, and she's stood by me for few years now. I'd been away for months at a time and she'd never complained, only given me her quiet and unrelenting support. Besides, it's better to be with her than on my own. And, it's all set, us having a baby and starting a family. It's a done thing.*

There was a sense of relief that things were moving in the right direction. He alighted at his stop and made his way to his apartment. Once inside he removed his coat then went to the bathroom to prepare for bed. When he walked into the bedroom he noticed the sleeping silhouette of Kate. Slight panic overtook him for a second, and he almost turned and fled. Instead he undressed and quietly got under the covers.

Kate moved towards him, still half-asleep, 'You're back,' she murmured. 'What took you so long?'

'I went to a dinner with a business partner. I didn't expect you'd come tonight. How are you feeling?'

Kate didn't answer; she had already gone back to sleep. Mark lay there for another ten minutes feeling the warmth of her body, which eventually lulled him to sleep.

He woke feeling a deep sense of satisfaction and turned to find Kate sleeping. This confused him, and he lay on his back for a minute, recalling his dream. In it, he was with Celine, feeling comfortable and secure with her although in the distance, he could see Kate walking away with their child looking very small in her arms...

Mark shrugged the dream off and put his arm around Kate, holding her close and feeling her still-flat belly, he held her tighter, as though trying to anchor himself to her. *This is real. Kate is real.*

Sarajevo, Bosnia, 1990s

Momir was feeling increasingly trapped; like a beast in a cage that nobody but the zookeeper visited. He had not ventured out for two years since the news that every male over the age of eighteen had to register for war services.

His mother was the main instigator for not allowing him show himself, and would often lie to anyone who asked. Her story was that Momir had moved to London with his mates, which was not impossible to believe.

Many of their neighbours were new, and as his mother would mention their names, and tell him what one or the other had said, or what their family situation was, Momir would try to imagine them. What did they look like? All those characters living barely a wall away who did not even know he lived next to them under the cover of his mother's watchful hen-like protection. The secrecy of the situation was the only way for him to survive. As far as the world knew, he did not exist.

Sometimes he felt like walking into the street and giving himself in just so he could talk to people. Maybe he should give himself up and gain a military position with the Bosnian army. *It cannot be worse than what I am living now.*

One morning he woke with a strong idea wedged in his mind. He decided to escape to the Serbian side of Bosnia. He had an aunt and uncle who had moved there at the very beginning of the war, and Momir hoped he could stay with them at first.

His mother was not so much against it, she even tried to get some more information about where the armed guards were, but having to remain secretive meant the information she gathered for Momir was more of a hindrance than help.

Ever since Momir hatched the idea to try and escape his mind refused to rest. He pulled some old maps of the city out of a cupboard where his primary school books were still stored – his mother had not wanted to get rid of them: 'They might come in handy, you never know.'

He watched the news, soaking in all the information about attacks and problems. He listened to the radio thinking any information was good information. Momir searched for information wherever he could: how to get out of here; how to cross over to the other side. Military police were on the streets, working in small groups stopping anybody who looked suspicious, or any men who looked healthy and over eighteen.

Momir watched the soldiers through the curtains as they passed under the window, machine guns hanging from their shoulders. Dressed in green camouflage uniforms, they moved silently in heavy black boots. They were the people he had to avoid at all costs.

He thought they would not be as careful around the time of intense attacks from Serbian positions, and they certainly would not be as careful during an attack. The best time to make a move would be just before dawn; he would be covered by the blanket of night, and yet should reach Serbian land before dawn. If he was caught, it would be by Serbs.

Days passed as he planned his escape, and for the first time in a long time, he felt alive. He felt he could change his life by going over to the other side. Be back amongst the living again.

What will I bring with me? What is important when escaping? He would have to walk maybe four hours before he found help. *I will need some food, and a flask of water.* There would be many springs in the forest where he could fill the bottle. *A blanket, it gets cold at night. Money. Yes I will need a bit of money. One hundred Deutschmarks will be enough. I just hope Mother will have that much to give me.* He would need a pack of cigarettes, too, but only to smoke when desperate. *That is all I need. Hmm, maybe some socks, extra socks, yes.*

Mother came to the door. 'Have you had anything to eat?'

'Yes, I had some bread and jam and a glass of milk.'

'You have been awfully quiet lately,' she said. 'We hardly talk anymore.'

Mother sat next to him. 'A neighbour was hurt when she went to get water from the pump. I met her daughter. She said her mother was taken to hospital with a head wound, but they did not keep her in. She was lucky; it was only...'

Momir stopped listening; he had heard these stories before, many times. They were the only stories he had heard since the beginning of the siege. Some stories were very bad, like when the high risers were bombed and a young couple were hit in their apartment – she lost both legs; he lost one. But the loss of faith in people was even bigger than that. The couple were both Serbs.

'...I need to go to the Red Cross to see if my sister has sent us a letter, hopefully—'

'Mum, I have decided,' Momir interrupted. 'I want to leave here.'

Mother went quiet. She froze, but finally uttered. 'I know. It's been two long years of this. This is no life. It doesn't matter for me, but you...'

'Mother, I am planning to escape,' he told her. 'I've worked out that the best way to do it... I will leave early in the morning, at least an hour or two before dawn breaks. I will give myself two hours—'

'If you are planning to do it then leave a couple of hours after midnight. You know Sarajevo like the palm of your hand. If you get out of it, even during nightfall, you will still know your way towards Serbian land.'

'You're right. I didn't think of that. Yes, you are right. I will leave a few hours after midnight; guards should be the least alert then.'

'When do you want to go?'

'In the next week'

A look of horror transformed his mother's face. 'That soon?' It appeared it was tough pronouncing those words, almost sapping all the energy from his mother's body. She slumped against the couch, her grey-streaked hair ruffled against the couch back rest. She carried on staring at Momir, but a slight smile of encouragement wove its way back to her face, and whilst her mind was somewhere else, Momir worried that the uncertainty surrounding his departure might disturb her even more.

London, UK, 1990s

Gina finally arrived back at her bedsit. She felt exhausted from the horrors taking place in her head. *Maybe I should see a doctor. I am not feeling well. I'll call Ian; he will help. He cares. Good old Ian.*

'Hello.' Ian's voice was dear and familiar.

'Ian. It's Gina. Could you come over? I am not feeling well. I've been walking all night... last night... and today. Please.'

'Gina, where are you? It is eleven o'clock at night.'

'Can I come to your place, Ian? I am not well. I think I need to go to the doctor.'

'God, Gina, I don't know. I'm working tomorrow morning. I'll come to your place and leave for work from there. Will you be okay?'

'I don't know. Just come as soon as you can, please.'

Ian arrived at her place within an hour and she was already in panic mode. 'Ian, I have been followed by two guys on the bus. I don't know what they want from me.'

'Gina, why would somebody follow you on the bus? It doesn't make sense.'

'I want to see a doctor.'

'Gina, I don't know where to find a doctor at this time of night. Can we do that tomorrow after I come back from work?'

Gina went quiet. 'Okay.'

Ian was already half asleep and just wanted to close his eyes. He fell asleep as soon as his head hit the pillow, but he was aware Gina hardly slept, although he was too tired to try and talk to her.

In the morning, Gina looked exhausted; dark rings sat under her eyes. 'You didn't sleep much, did you?'

Gina ignored his question. 'Do you want a coffee?'

It will do her good to do something. 'Yes, thank you, I would like a coffee.'

Gina left and Ian heard her in the downstairs kitchen. He was still dozing when he woke to a commotion from downstairs. Then he heard a man shriek: 'She is trying to kill me! Somebody help!'

Ian quickly slipped on his trousers and ran downstairs shirtless. Gina was standing in the middle of the communal kitchen wielding a jagged bread knife at a seemingly petrified landlord. The landlord was trembling, frozen in place. *Why has he come at this early hour*? 'What is going on?' Ian yelled. 'Gina, give me that knife, don't be stupid.'

Gina glared at him, and muttering something started towards the landlord as if to stab him.

'I'm calling the police.' The landlord turned and ran towards the main door.

'Please don't call the police,' Ian yelled after him. 'C'mon, you can't cut bread with this thing let alone hurt someone. Please stop!'

Thinking the landlord would just walk out and calm himself Ian turned towards Gina. She had already put the knife away and was running upstairs towards her room. Ian followed and found her sitting on her bed. 'That will teach him a lesson. Nasty little horror.'

'Gina, what did you do that for? What has he done to you?'

'If he thinks that I am going to sit and listen to his stories and take his degrading comments... well, no. He can give it to somebody else, not me, not me. I've had enough? Ha! He got scared! Uh, Gina you are mad! Ha, ha! Yes, I am mad, and you are clever.. and scared, ha ha...'

Suddenly three policemen stormed into the room, the landlord was behind them using the policemen like a shield. 'That's her, sitting on the bed! She tried to kill me!'

Ian was stunned. 'Why did you do this?' He looked in shock at the landlord. Then Ian turned to the policemen. 'This is just a misunderstanding. Please leave it, she is not feeling well.'

The policemen ignored him and begun manhandling Gina. Gina was resisting, of course, kicking her feet aimlessly. It did not take them long to have her in handcuffs. Ian looked on in disbelief. 'Where are you taking her?'

'To the police station,' one of the burly policeman replied. 'Where is the knife?'

'What knife? I don't know what you're talking about?' Ian said. 'But... all the knives are kept in the kitchen,' he added when the cop glared at him.

Ian walked into the kitchen hoping to see the knife first and kick it somewhere behind the fridge, but he could not see it. A moment later, one of the policemen began searching, too. With two of them in a small kitchen, it already felt crowded so Ian moved to the doorway to give the law space to do their job. It took some twenty minutes for the policeman to give up. 'I can't see it anywhere.'

'What will you do now?' Ian asked calmly, trying to establish some connection with the policeman.

The policeman ignored him and headed towards the front door.

'Where are you taking her?' Ian asked again.

'Marylebone Police Station,' was the only answer the policemen gave as he closed the back door of the van.

Ian could see Gina's face through the iron bars on the window, her eyes were glassy and distant.

Ian returned to the house, found the keys to her bedsit, put his shirt on, went to the bathroom to wash his face and clean his teeth before he went to work.

CHAPTER III

Celine felt elated the whole way home. *I have him in the palm of my hand*. The trip to Vienna would be a success. Just being with Mark, seeing him every day from morning till night would be bliss. She needed to have her hair done, her legs, and buy some gorgeous lingerie. Yes, she had to shop for clothes and bring her beautiful self to Vienna.

Celine noticed a man smiling at her on the bus, and she realised the man believed she was smiling at him, so she laughed softly to herself, then turned her gaze to the window. *London is beautiful at night. And I am part of it, I am part of that beauty; I belong here.*

Those same words she repeated before she fell into sweet, deserving sleep.

On Monday morning, Celine felt that the hard work on snaring Mark was only just beginning but she also knew she was strong enough to carry it through. She tried to catch a glimpse of Mark as she was sitting at her desk but his office was dark. *He must be coming in later,* she thought, and busied herself with work.

When she next looked up, she noticed the light in his office and her heart leapt in her chest. Now she had the perfect excuse to talk to him – their trip to Vienna. She had polished her project and was now ready to present it to him: cool, calm, competent, and a perfect companion for a trip to Vienna.

Celine snatched the opportunity around lunch when he was alone.

She walked into his office, acting as natural as possible as she approached him. 'Hi Mark, how are you?'

Mark looked up from his work. 'Oh Celine, yeah, I'm fine. Perfect timing. Please sit down.' He gave her a small smile. 'I've just spoken with the boss, and I've mentioned the Vienna trip, and he seems to be fine with it.'

Celine manufactured a perfect crown of confusion. 'Fine with...?'

'The two of us doing this project in Vienna. Or, are you not interested?' Mark was very business-like.

'Yes, sure I told you I would like to come, I mean I am interested in working with you, I mean this would be an excellent opportunity for me, I mean for business.'

A soft laugh lightened his features. 'You don't need to act all altruistic. It's a good project; and if I may, a few steps up the ladder for me too.'

Sarajevo, Bosnia, 1990s

The night was thick with smoke, remnants from gunfights in the surrounds of the city had broken late that afternoon. Eerie silence covered Sarajevo as Momir gazed through the window into the darkened street. Desolation ruled the street; hazy light from the very few street lamps, showed little of the gutted buildings, windowless frames and walls peppered with bullet holes.

Momir turned back to the room, his eyes finally resting on his rucksack. He felt his mother's presence; she stood frozen in the doorway. 'Mother, I am going tonight,' he said.

Silence.

'You know it is the right thing to do,' Momir said. 'I am dying slowly here.'

Mother just nodded.

Painfully aware that there was nothing else he could say to her, he started sifting through his small bag of belongings. 'I have everything I need here. I should get to the Serbs by the morning.'

'How much money do you have on you?'

'I'm fine. I have fifty German marks.'

'That's nothing.' His mother turned, heading to her secret stash.

'This is enough,' Momir called after her. 'I don't want any more!' Momir surprised himself with the resolution in his voice.

Mother stopped and walked back towards him, her eyes looking anywhere but at him. Momir could not prolong this agony any more, and fully aware that he had done all imaginable planning, he put his jacket on. Although it was warm, his jacket could double as a pillow or a blanket, survival might hinge on the smallest piece of equipment. His rucksack wasn't heavy. Should he be stopped, he would say he was going to see his aunt on the other side of the town to help her fix her broken window and other damage in her flat. The story was believable.

He walked to the door; his mother was not crying, but he knew her heart was about to shatter any moment. He hugged her tight. Her body was tense, and he could feel a river of tears frozen in her. He knew she would let them fall as soon as he was gone.

'You trust me, Mother, don't you?'

'Of course I do. You will be ok, you will make it my son. God bless you.'

Momir let go of his mother and walked out of the apartment quietly. He took one last look at her then with a faint smile he closed the door silently behind him. He walked down the stairs in the dark, then out of the building and into the warm May night.

London, UK, 1990s

Ian isolated himself from the others at his work, performing his job in a haze. He felt bad for leaving Gina alone at the police station, but she would be safe there.

Maybe she needs that kind of discipline. To be told that she is wrong by the law, by people who enforce order. She needs order.

Lunch was about to begin, so he immersed himself in the work.

'Could I please have those orders for table five? They've been waiting half an hour. They just complained that they need to go back to work.'

'Table seven waited for forty-five minutes; I need to do them first.' Chef was big and had his large spoon stuck into his breast pocket and a sachet of 'gold' saffron next to it.

'All right. But, please do table five immediately after. I'll let them know their lunch is on the way.'

Ian backed through the swinging door into the restaurant and scanned the tables and the customers looking for any sign of dissatisfaction or a call for service.

'Excuse me, over here young man.' A customer in a striped suit motioned him over.

'Yes, sir. How can I help?' Ian said as he approached the table.

'I did not get my side dish of vegetables with my lunch. Could you see to it, please?'

'Certainly, sir.'

Ian went to the kitchen and took a hot side dish plate from the warmer and offered it to one of the sous chefs. 'Table twenty-three didn't get their side dish of vegetables. Could you please do one now so I can take it to him before he finishes his lunch?'

The sous chef did as asked with some grumbling under the breath. 'We wouldn't let a dinner plate go out without a side dish. Impossible. One of the waiters took it to the wrong table. Useless they are.'

'Thanks, Barry. I appreciate it.' Ian ignored the sous chef's comments and took the side dish out to the customer with a smile and an apology.

Ian cleaned a few extra glasses off the table making sure the customers were aware he was taking care of them. Another gentleman called him as he was heading towards the kitchen. 'Could I please have another glass of wine?'

'Certainly, sir. What was the wine?'

'Sancerre. It's a fine drop.'

'Good choice, sir.'

As he went to the bar, he noticed the dessert trolley being pushed to a table as they finished their main meal. *Service is ending. I need it.*

He waited as the customer emptied his glass, whisked it away and returned with a fresh glass. Ian turned as he overheard a customer ask his waiter about the dessert trolley. 'So, what would you suggest, young man?'

'Oh, I'd go for a tart sir, any time.'

Only Paul could get away with a comment like that to a regal-looking gentleman in his sixties. The man had a slight smile on his face as he ordered bread and butter pudding, which probably reminded him of his Eton school days.

Ian answered a few more calls as customers were slowly beginning to leave; some back to work, and some no doubt on to more drinking.

Waiters begun to clear away the tables while Ian went from the bar to the restaurant and back to make sure the final jobs were finished, and the tables were prepared for the dinner crowd. He wasn't working for dinner service, which meant it was time to go and see Gina.

When he finally returned to the change room, he felt tired but decided not to go home first.

'You're off this evening. What are you up to?' Paul asked with a cheeky grin.

'Staying in,' Ian told him. 'I have some study to do.'

'Always study. Go and chase some girls, Ian. It'll do you good.' Paul threw his bag over his shoulder. 'See you tomorrow. You're up at breakfast?'

Ian shook his head. 'No. I'm on breakfast the day after tomorrow. See you then.'

As Ian sat in the tube on the way to Marylebone, all the anguish of the previous night and this morning came crashing back. And it didn't get any better as he approached the police station.

'I am looking for a woman called Gina,' Ian said to the policewoman sitting at the front desk. 'She was brought in this morning. Would I be able to get some information about her?'

'Gina, yes. Are you a relative?'

'I am her friend. She does not have any relatives in London,' Ian told the policewoman.

'Does she have a history of mental health issues? She was acting quite strangely this morning and has been taken to a hospital to be assessed by a psychiatrist.' The policewoman looked at Ian and then repeated. 'She was taken to a hospital to be assessed by a psychiatrist.'

Melbourne, Australia, 2000s

It was three o'clock Saturday afternoon when Tanya closed the agency and put the keys into her bag, feeling slightly proud that she was already trusted to close the office. After stopping for groceries on her way home, Tanya's thoughts turned to Goran. *I like him. I like that he is from my old country. We have lots in common... and he is good looking.*

When she arrived home and began taking her shopping out of the boot, she heard voice behind her.

'Hi Tanya.' Her neighbour was approaching her car.

Tanya smiled. 'Hi Kelly. How're you doing?'

'I'm off to hen's party. My friend Marianne... have I told you about her? Well, she's having a 70s themed party. How do you like my hair?' Before Tanya could respond, her neighbour continued. 'Anyway, it's in this bar in the city called Rumba. Have I told you about it? Well, you get there, they give you a coupon, and like ... then you keep drinking, and at the end of the night you just pay your bill. I mean it's so classy. And, the music is, like, a mix of hip-hop and groove with some lounge as well. I am going to dance my tush off. How about you?'

Tanya shrugged. 'I just finished work...'

'You work on Saturday? That's so depressing. I can't remember when I last worked on Saturday. Oh, maybe when I was in Sydney, in that bar, have I told you about that bar? Actually, I have to go. See you later. Bye.'

Tanya felt slightly nauseated after that conversation. Kelly would always leave her feeling as if her life was dull. Now in such an unpleasant mood she started unloading her bag onto the kitchen bench when her phone rang. She answered.

'Hi, remember me?'

'Hmm, if you say your name, I might remember you?' Tanya said.

'It's Goran.'

Tanya's lips opened wide into a large smile. 'Hi, of course I remember you. What are you up to?'

'I thought we could meet and have a coffee tomorrow?' Goran's voice seemed filled with excitement.

'Of course.' Tanya felt light enough to float. 'That would be good. Where do you want to meet?'

'Maybe we could meet somewhere at your end,' Goran said, his voice deep and smooth. 'There are more cafes there.'

'Sure, but I am new here, so I don't know many places.'

'Ok, let's meet on the corner of Farraday and Smith Street tomorrow,' Goran said decisively.

'What time? Around five?' Tanya was guessing.

'Could we make it six? I have to pick up some stuff from a friend.'

'Yes, sure. Six is fine.'

'Then see you at six.'

She put the phone down, and her fears seemed to fly away. Her insecurities were wiped like they never had existed. Goran was quite a good looking man, and if he called so soon that meant he must be interested in her and she wanted to look her best when she met him. What will I wear?

She opened the door to her wardrobe and looked pitifully at the pieces hanging there. She would not wear a skirt, that was far too formal. Possibly trousers... jeans were too common a choice. Light brown, low-cut trousers looked fine. Now for the top. A shirt looked too official... possibly a white top and brown loafer shoes. Yes. Nice and relaxing, yet classy. She tried it on and felt comfortable with the way she looked.

Her mood lifted, and she marvelled at how quickly it disappeared so that she could not even recall feeling down anymore. She started preparing lunch, mixed some minced meat, peeled and cut potatoes then put everything into the oven. As she was preparing her salad her cat purred as it rubbed herself against her legs.

'What's the matter? Are you hungry, Milica?'

Milica looked at her, squinted her eyes, and rubbed her body along Tanya's legs again, then lifted her tail and strolled to her bowl.

'Sorry, Milica, I forgot to buy your food. Milk will have to do for today.'

Milica dragged herself over and started slurping her milk then went to the armchair and nestled herself into a nice little ball and started purring as she snoozed. Tanya turned on the television; some art programs were on, and she flicked through the channels then checked the TV guide but soon abandoned the idea and grabbed a magazine instead.

Tanya was going to the cinema with a friend tonight, she hardly knew anybody from her country who now lived in Australia, just a few people who she knew through work and were much older than she and not really appropriate for her to socialise with. At forty-one, her age felt burdensome in many different ways. If she had been back home, she would have been called "past it". Here, age was not a big issue, but the two cultures were mixing in her head. Instead of rationally taking the best from each, she felt inappropriate in most social circles. Sometimes it was as though her age was dragging her down and her future seemed uncertain, except... this call today showed a small ray of hope.

Her one long relationship kept coming back to haunt her even after sixteen years. Tanya did not know where Nenad was or if he was missing her at all. She had been finishing university when they'd met. It had been like a lightning strike their meeting and time together afterwards, like walking into a place bathed in the sun. They'd met in spring: days were longer, nights warmer. She had been somebody different then – confident, precocious – she believed in herself and her powers to have what she wished for. Her confidence was based on her youth. She'd enjoyed spending time with Nenad. He would call often – that, she took for granted. Later she had realised he had taken her for granted, too. War had hung in the air like bad perfume loitering on the edges of their existence. Tanya felt uneasy about the future in the country, but she'd been lost for words on how to explain the feeling of insecurity and danger that persisted around her. He had been oblivious, as if they were in the peace-loving 70s, and not the late-80s and a time of change. He persisted in going out, enjoying their youth while she'd wanted to stay in and wait for God knew what.

Sarajevo, Bosnia, 1990s

Kemal and Selma were none the wiser the morning they received that phone call. Sunlight, oblivious to the war, danced across the room reflecting off the credenza's glass. Selma's face was a blank canvas for the sun's mischievous game, but she continued to sit still by Kemal's feet. Kemal held his beads, murmuring his prayers as if the hours did not pass at all. Selma was scratching the kilim[5] on which she sat, collecting a few invisible pieces of dirt before she stood.

'Father, do you want a coffee?'

'Yes, Selma, my daughter, please bring me a coffee. It will give you something to do,' Kemal said watching Selma. She looked far older than her forty-three years; a few new grey hairs were glittering as they escaped from beneath the scarf.

'I will call Mehmed's family, he is in the same unit as your son and husband; they might have some more news. Bring me the phone, Selma,' said Kemal and then dialled the number and waited for a reply. It was seven in the morning, maybe a little bit early, but...

'Hello.'

'Hello, it is Kemal here. Is that you Suljo? Sorry to call this early. I hope I haven't woken anybody.'

'Kemal, we hardly ever sleep, and anyway somebody is always awake. '

'Have you heard any news from Mehmed?'

---

5   Kilim – thin hand-woven carpet common in Bosnian households

'They called us from the command and told us that Mehmed's unit was cut off. Your son and grandson were there too, weren't they? Have you had any more news?'

'No, same as you, just that they were cut off,' Kemal said with a sigh.

'I will go to the town today and try to learn some more. If I find out anything I'll let you know.' Suljo sounded concerned about his son.

'Thanks. May Allah be with you,' Kemal piously added.

'Selam Kemal. May Allah be with you, too.'

Selma returned with his coffee. 'Any news, Father?'

'Nothing Selma, nothing. They know nothing about Mehmed either,' Kemal told her. 'Selma, dear, I will go to the mosque today.'

'All right, Father, do as you have to.'

Kemal put on his coat and left the house. The air in the street was filled with smoke and dust. He did not know some of the people now living in the street as they had moved in from the local villages and into the abandoned houses. Some were from the Serbian side of Bosnia and were given some sort of papers that allowed them to stay in the houses.

Kemal could hardly recognise the street anymore. Only glimpses of the old were coming from the corners of his memory. Houses were now scarred from sniper shots and shells shattering against the walls, some roofs were damaged, and makeshift UN tarpaulins were stretched to protect the rooms underneath from snow and rain.

When Kemal arrived at the mosque, there were some outside washing their hands, face and feet and he slowly removed his shoes and washed one foot then the other. After he dried his feet, he put on the slippers provided, and shoes in hand, he walked towards the door of the mosque.

Placing his shoes with the other pairs; he took off the slippers and entered the mosque. He kneeled on the carpet and started praying. He thought of his son and grandson. *Where are they now? Please Allah deliver them back to us well. Allah almighty, look after them.*

'C'mon people, don't take too long, it is not a good time to stay in the mosque for too long. You all know that. Chetniks[6] won't leave us alone especially in here.' The voice of the young cleric broke through Kemal's prayers and he got slowly to his feet and headed towards the exit, where he bumped into Hodza.

'Selam[7], Hodza.'

'Ah Kemal, Selam to you. How's your family?'

'Not well, my dear Hodza, my son and grandson were in the unit that was cut off due to heavy fighting with Serbs.'

'That's terrible Kemal, have you tried to find out more?'

'I don't know who to ask. Where do I go? The army's Headquarters rang us, but I just do not know.'

'Go home, Kemal,' Hodza told him gently. 'I see many people here, and I will try and find out more. If I have any information, I will call you.'

Kemal gave Hodza his phone number, hoping that the man would be able to help.

---

6 Chetnik – member of the organization of Serbian fighters started in the first half of the 20th century
7 Selam – traditional greeting among Muslims, word of Turkish origin

'Thanks Kemal, you were one of the first I met when I began my service at this mosque, long before this zulum[8] happened. Go, and Selam to you, Kemal.'

Kemal kissed Hodza's hand and he pushed him slightly as though trying to lessen this good deed.

Once outside, Kemal sat on a small bench and put his shoes on. This place filled him with much hope and peace that he could not find anywhere else. *God the almighty, let my kids live, take my life instead. Spare them, I beg of you.*

He looked up at the sky, the sun was a big orange smudge. He felt a warm tear on his cheek, and he brushed it off with the palm of his hand.

'Are you still here, Kemal?' It was Hodza. 'Kemal, we don't gather anywhere for too long. The enemy is close by, and they hit at us whenever we are in groups. You should know that. Go home, in Allah's name. Leave.'

'I know, Hodza, I know. But, by Allah I love it here. May sheitan[9] take them to hell. Allahmanet[10], Hodza.'

'Alahmanet, Kemal.'

London, UK, 1990s

Celine was elated after the conversation with Mark; the trip to Vienna had been her *coup d'état*. She now had to plan it to the minute detail and ensure she was confident

---

8   Zulum – bad times, word of Turkish origin
9   Sheitan – devil, word of Turkish origin
10 Alahmanet – goodbye and God bless you, word of Turkish origin

and prepared for any eventualities. Things could go wrong, but her confidence would see her through.

Mark's secretary would organise Celine's plane ticket, all she had to worry about was packing all her saucy clothes. If only her friends from the old country could see her now, all up-and-coming. Successful.

They were leaving in two weeks' time; she needed to see a beautician, then it would be shopping, shopping and some more shopping over the weekend. Her phone rang, and Celine thought not to answer, but the ringing was persistent. 'Hello?'

'Hi Celine, it's me, Ian. Listen, some terrible things have happened with Gina… she was arrested this morning, they have now sent her to a general hospital, mental ward. I think it would be a good idea if you went to see her.'

'Ian, wait, slow down. Gina's in a hospital? Or she will be in a mental hospital? What has she done? What is going on?' Celine shook her head and continued. 'But then she's always been a bit weird. That might fix her up.'

'Can you go and see her and talk to her? I am at my wit's end. I don't know what to tell her.'

'Ian, I'm busy at the moment, I've got a business trip to Vienna coming up. I have to go. I don't have time for Gina and her silly, wasteful lifestyle.' Celine felt a sense of importance as she uttered the words.

'You're a woman; you have a better understanding.' Ian sounded desperate.

I am a woman all right, and I am just about to use my last morsels of it, but for my own advantage, not Gina's. What has she ever done for me? And Ian's not giving up.

'Ok, Ian, I'll talk to her. Which hospital is she in? God, if someone sees me going there, it will be severely embarrassing! Gina is a nightmare, honestly!'

'I know, I know. Just please talk to her. She hasn't been admitted yet, but in a day or two they will move her, she is being assessed by a psychiatrist in one hospital. It's just across the road from Charring Cross tube station. You can't miss it. Celine, you are a hero! Thanks a lot for doing this. You know, her mother would be devastated if she knew.'

'Gina's mother doesn't know anything about this?! What is wrong with you? Call her mother and talk to her!'

'Celine, I can't. It would kill her. You don't understand how fragile that woman is. There's a war going on over there. There is no war in your part of the country; your family is relatively safe. It is terrible in Bosnia at the moment. We'll get Gina out of this mess and then she can talk to her.'

Celine sighed dramatically.

'Let Gina talk to her mother when she gets better and can settle things for herself. Please, Celine.'

He is desperate to be begging me like this. 'Okay, no problem. I'll go. I have to go now. Bye.'

Ian

Ian felt slight relief. Another woman would probably understand Gina better. He was lost with all her problems. He didn't know what to say most of the time, and that was of no help to her. As it was already late Ian planned on going to the hospital in the morning, so he settled down to watch some television, but he was restless. He tried a book, then a magazine before going to a chest where all his photographs were kept.

He found a photograph of him and Gina when she was about four years old, and he at about six. She was in shorts and a light cream t-shirt; he was in overall-shorts with a pocket at the top, large straps across his tiny shoulders. Although not related, he had his arm around her, like protective big brother. She had been his charge; he had looked after her, kept her safe since they were kids. He did not feel that he was keeping her safe now. Rules had changed; it wasn't as easy anymore, and he felt powerless to make changes in Gina's life anymore.

It was close to midnight when he finally went to bed and he was pleased he did not have to work the next day. Tomorrow would be dedicated to finding the hospital where Gina had been moved; he needed to reassure her that everything would be okay.

He spent the next hour tossing and turning, unable to sleep. He also needed to return Carol's call – she wanted him to help her move house on Sunday. Ian had thought of asking her to move in together, but was still not sure how he felt about her. She was sweet sometimes, and with her being English, if he married her it would solve his residency-status.

Besides, he was not sure if she was totally faithful to him. The path he was on with Carol was promising as her presence filled him with joy, and a future with her seemed bright. There was a sense of stability and fullness about her. She had an aura of un-attainability, and he was always left wanting more. He loved her rust-coloured hair, freckles sprinkled around her small, upturned nose. Her smile was bright, so knowing and mysterious. She seemed to embody the perfect woman he and his mate Momir admired as they watched foreign films sprawled on the couch, drinking beer. This thought made him smile. Carol was his teenage dream.

Ian woke from an uneasy dream. Carol was hugging some English, yuppie-looking guy while sheepishly looking at Ian. He went to the bathroom washing away that thought and the feeling before finding the name of the hospital where Gina was. It was an easy trip on the tube.

He found the hospital easily and was waiting for the mental-health care nurse to take him to Gina. Elbows resting on his knees, head down, he spotted a white pair of shoes marching towards him. He sat upright as a middle-aged woman with salt-and-pepper hair and tightly-fitted blue uniform walked briskly towards him. He stood when she approached.

'Hello. Are you relative of Gina?'

'No, but I am her friend, a childhood friend. I know her family, but they don't live in England.'

The nurse nodded sharply. 'Gina had a restless sleep last night. She's been assessed and will be transferred to a more permanent mental facility outside London.' The nurse was very business-like. 'She will be sectioned under the mental health law for three months at a mental health institution.'

Ian could not believe what he was hearing. 'You can't do that. She won't be able to stand it. She will go mad.'

The nurse suddenly smiled softly at Ian. 'Miss Gina is not well, young man. She has been accused of making serious threats toward somebody with a knife. She'll be here for treatment. She is a lucky girl, in a way.'

Ian did not know what to do, but this was something nobody would know how to deal with. It was Gina's choice to reveal that about her life. 'Okay, thanks,' Ian said politely. 'Can I talk to Gina now?'

'Certainly, I will show you to her bed. Don't get too upset, she has some bruises on her face and arms as she was fighting the male nurses and had to be restrained and sedated last night. She is still very antagonistic.'

When he walked into Gina's hospital room all he could see was white. White floors, white walls, white beds... and there, Gina, surrounded by that whiteness. He became aware of a few more patients in other beds near the window, but his focus remained on Gina, lying in her bed and very alert.

Her bed was a white painted iron, white sheet and white bedspread with a white blanket on top. Her white pillows were propped at her back, and Gina was looking around the room as if expecting an attack.

'Ian! Thanks for coming.'

'How are you?' he asked then quickly realised his mistake. 'Ah, do you want me to keep quiet about this?' *Another thing I should not have said.*

'Who would you be talking to about this?' She seemed quite aware of her surroundings and situation. 'I want to get out of here, the sooner the better.'

But then again, maybe not. Maybe she was not so aware of what was going on. 'Gina, the nurse told me they'll keep you in an institution for three months.'

Gina stared; her jaw dropped. 'You must be *joking!* I am not staying in this place for three months!'

'It won't be here. They'll move you to a hospital outside London,' Ian said as gently as he could.

'I am not sick,' Gina said firmly. 'I don't want to be in a hospital.'

'You don't have choice, Gina. They told me you'll get hospital instead of prison.'

'Prison? For what?' then Ian saw the memory return to Gina's eyes. 'Oh, for attacking that idiot.'

'Why did you do it, Gina?' Ian finally asked.

'He's a cretin! He was constantly annoying me!'

'Well, annoy him back! You don't need to go to the extreme!'

Gina fell into silence, acting as though he was already gone. He watched as she stared blankly then the light came back to her eyes and she finally turned her gaze back to him. 'How's your work? How's Carol? Are you still together?'

'Ah, everything's fine. Will you be okay here?' he asked but he needed to reassure her. 'I will come to see you in the new hospital. I promise.'

'What new hospital? I am leaving here in a couple of days. Could you bring me a fresh set of clothes from my flat? Just call my landlord; he'll give you the keys.'

'I have the keys,' he said as he stood. 'I'll go now, Gina. Please look after yourself, and I'll bring you the clothes. Is there anything else you need?'

'Ian, I want to get out of here,' she said. 'Go and talk to those horrible nurses! I am not staying here!'

Ian tried to hug her, but she pushed him away.

'What is wrong with you? Get away from me. Why are you feeling sorry for me?'

'No, I don't feel sorry for you,' he said. *I feel sorry for myself.* 'I'll see you soon'

A terrible feeling of powerlessness overcame him as he walked out on Gina.

CHAPTER IV

Melbourne, Australia, 2000s

When Tanya met Goran that evening, he suggested they go to a café. Conversation flowed easily between them and Goran was paying her a lot of attention; it was as though there was nobody else but the two of them there. She felt comfortable, and thought for a moment how everything that was wrong with her previous relationships was now forgotten. She could not remember feeling angry or depressed. It was all wiped out as she sat with Goran.

'Have you been in Australia long?' Tanya asked.

'About eight years. How about you?'

'I've been here for a year only. Are you pleased that you made the choice to come over?'

Goran took a sip of his coffee then looked to her. 'I wouldn't have met you if I didn't?' he grinned cheekily.

Tanya blushed. 'True.'

Goran was going away for two weeks the following day, and they arranged to meet again when he returned.

He sent SMS messages, and called her once. The last message was to confirm when they would meet and where. Tanya was delighted. Goran thought of her and wanted to see her again – it was a good sign.

As she pondered this, her landline rang. She quickly went to the phone and answered it.

'Hi, it's Kelly.'

'Hi. How're you doing?'

'Ever since you started seeing that guy from your old country I haven't seen you. What's going on?'

'I don't know. I can't tell.' Tanya thought about 'the relationship' for the first time since it began. 'I think it is okay, but...'

'But...?'

'I think he likes me. He calls a lot. We do have good conversations.'

'And the rest? Do you like him?'

'I do,' Tanya said. 'I like spending time with him. But I still haven't seen him much. We talk on the phone a lot though.'

'That's bit strange. Why don't you ask him why?'

'I find it strange that he hasn't introduced me to any of his friends. Now that he's away, I feel completely isolated from his life'.

'You don't know any of his friends? That is really strange,' Kelly said. 'Do you want to talk? Do you want me to come over for a cup of coffee?'

'No, I have to go out this evening and I have things to do beforehand. I think we are fine. I am just being overly sensitive.'

'Well, I find it strange that I haven't seen him come to your place at all.'

'He will.'

'By now, I would be all over him,' Kelly said with a laugh.

'We don't know each other that well.' Tanya answered without thinking.

'What's there to know? Is he good looking? Grab him and bring him in like a proper cave woman.'

Tanya laughed. 'I don't know about that.'

'I'll come to the wedding.'

'I don't know about that either,' Tanya said. 'We've only just started the relationship.'

'Okay, well let me know how it all works out. Bye'

'Bye.'

Tanya shook her head as she hung up the phone. *I'll come to the wedding. Cave woman. How stupid is that! I should have told her something. She is having me on! Why didn't I say something? Goran is just leading me on? Nothing will eventuate from this. Does something need to eventuate?*

Tanya smiled. *Well, it does. I'll talk to him about this. What will I tell him? Bottom line is: do I want to start a relationship with him? Yes, I do. Other women wouldn't let things be this way. They would plan something. But do I want to be with him?*

Tanya started looking for her mobile phone. *I'll ask him by SMS what his plans are with me.* She stopped, reflecting for a moment. *His plans with me? What are his plans with me!? That's stupid! I need to formulate it better. I will. I can't listen to Kelly.*

Tanya sat on the couch with a sigh. *Kelly doesn't have the same mentality as me. She was born into a different culture. I can't go with her ideas. Not if I am going out with somebody from my old country. It is different between us. It is a different set of rules. Kelly is just being friendly. She has been helpful and supportive in fact. I need to have my own opinion on this. Do I like Goran? Do I want to be with him? Why did he ask me out and then leave me to go away somewhere?* Tanya looked through the window into distance. *Maybe he had to.*

Tanya did some chores to calm herself, then read a book before tossing through some magazines. She finally re-read Goran's message. *He does like me and everything will be fine.*

Sarajevo, Bosnia, 1990s

Momir had a vague plan on which was the best way to leave Sarajevo in order to reach Serbian positions safely. He only carried a small rucksack, which wouldn't look suspicious even if somebody opened it – people carried rucksacks like that with pieces of meat or bread and even socks for relatives, all the time.

The streets were filled with shadows, the street lamps standing battered and useless. Momir scanned his surroundings. Nobody was in sight. The streets were eerily quiet. Buildings ravaged by gunfire loomed like giant monsters from a nightmare.

Momir's heart raced as he crossed the street and took shelter beside a large tree. He calmed his breathing then snapped his head to sudden movement on the right; a soldier in Bosnian army uniform some fifty meters in front and heading his way.

He had to move. *There*. Keeping low, he ran to the ruins of a house that sat like a decayed tooth in the street. He squatted behind its walls, breathing heavily.

Steps scraped louder. Closer. Momir's heart leapt to his throat. Part of him wanted to jump in front of the soldier and yell: 'Here I am! Do with me what you wish!' But self-preservation and fear held him in place. As the soldier's footsteps faded, relief flooded through Momir – he'd won this small battle. He carefully poked his head around the wall; the soldier was already a shadow in the distance.

Hunched, Momir ran silently across the street; taking left turns and right, he moved through the neighbourhood, trying to blend into his surroundings while conscious of every sound. But there was no sound, not even the hum of insects disturbed the night. All he could hear was his heart thumping in his chest.

Another house rose from the shadows. Overgrown grass reached like a thousand fingers up to its glassless windows. It was eerily dark, and he remembered all the stories of old witches, vampires and other nightmare creatures. The stories didn't seem as funny now as they had then. *Just press on.*

The railway was just up ahead, and he made sure not to step on the tracks; sound passed down the line faster than it would through air. His breathing was loud in his ears; his heart pounding: *thump, thump, thump.* Momir was sure it echoed around the whole area.

The foot of the mountain wasn't far but it felt like an eternity away. Just one more hill and he would be at the bottom of Trebevic.

'Hey, you! What are you doing here?'

Momir froze. *This can't be happening.* His whole body was in spasm, and he turned as if in a dream. Three soldiers stood close enough that he could clearly see their shabby Bosnian army uniforms. Two were taking the guns from their shoulders, and Momir's gut clenched at the sound of metal scraping against fabric.

'What's in the rucksack? Are you deaf?' spat a small, wiry soldier.

'I am going to see my aunt,' Momir said as calmly as he could. 'She lives near Debelo Brdo.'

'Yeah, and I am a big scary wolf who will eat you and your aunt,' the same soldier scoffed.

The other two soldiers laughed, the sound grating on the still night air.

'The only thing missing is a red hood,' the first soldier continued.

'Give us your papers,' a big, burly-looking soldier demanded.

Momir reached into his jacket and removed papers his mother had managed to get for him. He could do nothing except hand the papers over and hope they passed scrutiny.

'Momir. You're a Chetnik, ha.' The big, tough looking soldier spoke with an accent of a villager.

'Chetnik going to his aunty into the woods,' added the wiry soldier; his beard and moustache were barely grown in.

The third soldier was quiet, his head down, as though he didn't want to be there. 'Let him go. Who cares.'

'I care!' the big soldier spat. 'We fight, while this Chetnik walks around like he has no care in the world. I bloody care!'

The quiet soldier looked resigned 'So what do you want to do?'

'Do you know,' started the big soldier as he turned to Momir, 'that we could kill you and nobody would ever find out who finished you off? There is so much shit going on that one more body splattered across the lines won't make any difference.'

Momir hesitated, but saying nothing wouldn't help him. 'I know that you could just kill me,' Momir said softly, 'but I am just going to see if my aunt survived the shelling.' *I am at their mercy. My powers are zero.*

'How about we do the right thing then,' the soldier said. 'We will take you to our commander.' Turning to the other two soldiers, he inclined his head 'What do you think? Is that the right thing to do?'

The other two looked at Momir, then scanned the area before the wiry soldier said 'That is a very big gesture from you.'

The quiet one remained silent.

'What do you think Mirza?' the big soldier asked.

'If you think that's the right thing to do, let's do it. You are the boss.'

'All right, let's go.' The big soldier pushed Momir ahead of them. 'And don't even think about running. You'd only be doing us a favour.'

Kemal

The door opened slowly before Kemal. Selma's expression was sad and desperate. 'Did you learn anything about where they are?'

'No, I didn't,' Kemal said gently. 'But I did talk to Hodza and he's promised to let me know if he finds out anything.' Kemal removed his shoes and put on slippers before walking into the lounge room. 'Have you eaten something Selma?'

'No, I was waiting for you,' she replied. 'Are you hungry? Shall we have some breakfast now?'

'Sure. You should not have waited for me. I am old. It doesn't matter if I miss a meal or two.'

'I've baked bread out of the last bits of flour we had and our neighbour gave us some oil as I didn't have any left.'

'After we eat I will go to the Merhamet[11] and see if we could get some oil and flour. Do we have any sugar?'

Kemal sat on the couch listening to Selma bustle around in the kitchen. The phone rang and Kemal heard Selma's footsteps race to the phone, and moments later she called him.

'Kemal speaking. Yes, that's me. I understand. Yes. Yes. I see. We can do that. Yes, certainly. We will be there. First of November, you said. At eleven am, yes, at the border. Thank you. Thank you, so much. Do you know, if they are well? No problem, I understand. Thank you. Good bye.'

---

11   Merhamet – humanitarian organization for Muslims in Bosnia

Kemal put the phone down and turned to Selma. 'They have found them. They will be exchanged on the first of November at the border. Oh, Selma, this is such good news. They are alive!'

Kemal grabbed Selma and held her so tight that she started feeling breathless not knowing if it was from the happiness and relief that her husband and son were alive, or from Kemal's bear hug. Everything looked different now. This flat wasn't so empty, colours returned and Selma noticed the sun outside.

She went to the window and looked into the sky. 'Look Kemal. It is sunny.' She caught her reflection in the glass, and pulled her scarf forward as some hair was showing.

'Selma, you are being silly now.'

Selma just waved and kept staring at the beauty of a day over the devastated city. When she turned away from the window, Kemal was looking at the calendar. 'What day is the first?' Selma asked.

'Wednesday,' he said. 'The day after tomorrow.'

'Do you know the exact spot where the exchange will happen?'

'At the foot of Debelo Brdo. A few kilometres past the old railway station.'

'Will we be able to find it?' Selma asked. 'Serbs won't shoot at us, will they?'

'No, the UN peacekeepers will be there, and all the newspapers, too. It is a big thing.'

'So we won't miss it. We will find the place.'

'Of course,' Kemal reassured.

'Should I bring a change of clothes for them?' Selma asked.

'That will be the last thing on their mind. But, maybe you could bring a couple of shirts, just so they feel they are home.'

'It will take us an hour to walk there,' Selma said. 'Our neighbour has not heard about her husband and he was taken about the same time as our boys. Shall I let her know about our news?'

'Don't!' Kemal said more harshly than intended. 'Who knows what happened with her husband. If there is any news she will let you know.'

'You are right. It would be awful if I told her that ours are coming home and she still has not heard.'

'Of course.' Kemal smiled. 'Make them burek on Sunday.'

'Yes, they will love it. But you have to get flour and oil. And meat. Shall I go?'

'No, don't. While I am alive I'll go out.' His smile widened. 'Oh, Selma what a good day today is. Thank you Allah, thank you from the bottom of my heart. I will repay you. I am enslaved to you for the rest of my life. Inshallah.'

All Saturday night Selma did not sleep well. She dozed on and off until exhaustion finally claimed her as dawn broke.

Her dream was strange. She was at the old railway station and her husband and son were standing there. Her son then crossed the railway line to her side. She held him, kissed him and then stared across the line at where Seid was standing a moment ago. The station was deserted.

Selma woke uneasy and looked at the clock – seven already. She dressed quickly and walked into the lounge room to find Kemal sitting in a cloud of cigarette smoke and having a coffee.

'You are up already? Did you sleep well?' Selma asked.

'Not very well. I kept thinking of them. Will we find them well?'

'I haven't slept well either. I'll just have a coffee and and then maybe we go? I have prepared the change of clothes and some food for them. Everything is ready.'

Selma and Kemal walked quietly next to each other. Her father-in-law had slowed with age, he was nearing eighty, but held his head high. They walked across the now dead tram lines; the sound of trams running just a distant memory. It was Wednesday morning and there were few people on the streets. The sombre look on their faces was the most common thing about them. One could offer a fortune for a smile but it would go unpaid.

They passed a block of flats totally ravaged by shelling and gunfire. Windows were none existent, and the inner walls were now exposed to weather. The whole area looked like carnage. Still, people lived here.

There were many new people living in the neighbourhood, but most only went out to buy basics. There were black markets, of course, but that was okay, these were abnormal times. Normality would roll in again. Three years of bad times felt like thirty years of misery.

As they walked through the rubble of Sarajevo, they passed the bench where she and Seid had first kissed twenty years ago, and a warm flush rushed through her. Seid had been walking her home and had asked her to sit and enjoy the summer night with him. She remembered it like it was yesterday. Stars sparkled in the inky sky, a warm breeze brushing her skin. They sat demurely and slightly lost for words as they both knew what was coming but didn't quite know where to start. Seid had started with a few slightly clumsy words then put his hand on hers, as though testing the terrain. Selma did not pull her hand away. He turned to her and touched her lips gently with his.

Selma trembled at the thought of that kiss. *How many things has that one kiss started in her life?* She did not regret any of it. He was a good man. They had a good marriage. She only wished they had another child, a daughter. It hadn't happened, but she hoped it still would. And Seid's mother always blamed Selma for the fact.

'My son should have had a school of children. Not just one.'

The words hurt, and they still gnawed at her, made her feel inadequate. Maybe the universe will help her conceive again, even in these hard times.

'Pray, Selma. Now that you are here in our house to stay. Pray that I get at least one more grandchild.' Selma's mother-in-law was relentless.

Selma would get angry at this but could not say anything to her mother-in-law as this would turn her husband against her. So she had put on a brave face and suffered in silence. But now that her mother-in-law was not alive anymore, Selma did not feel much guilt for complaining to her girlfriends about the woman. She could not even complain to her own family as her mother would surely have shut her down with one sentence: *'They took you into their home!'* As if she came off the street or something.

Her father was a quiet man. He'd died just after she met Seid. Her father worked as a steam engine coal loader, he was always covered in black soot. She loved the smell on his clothes when she would put her head into his lap while her mother was preparing him a warm bath. 'Get off of me, I'll dirty your pretty white dress,' her father would say with a smile, but would never push her. It was her mother when she'd caught her with black dust down her dress that would cuss her: 'I don't have six pairs of hands to wash you, you little daddy's princess.' Her father liked Seid, and that was of great consolation to her. Kemal reminded her of her father.

Selma and Kemal were approaching the railway station – the line of division between Muslims and Serbs. This was where the exchange of war prisoners was to take place. Selma worried at what she would find. How would her son and husband look? Her father-in-law coughed a bit and when Kemal coughed again, Selma slowed her step. 'Do you feel tired? Do you want to sit down for a moment? We have a whole hour before it starts.'

Selma was bit troubled knowing that her father-in-law must be overwhelmed; as his age, too many emotions could be devastating to his health.

'No, push on,' Kemal said. 'We will sit when we get there. It is only another fifteen minutes away.'

Selma knew it was a bit longer but there was no point in arguing. Just like her father.

They were walking across fields covered in overgrown grass and spotted with sporadic blotches of red, yellow and purple flowers. She had played here as a child. An old house sat in the grassland, completely ravaged by shells. There was no roof – just the bullet-riddled walls surrounding weeds and rugged bushes. She remembered people living in that house and wondered what had happened to them.

Kemal interrupted her thoughts. 'We need to be very careful walking around here. There might be snakes hiding in this undergrowth. Let's move to that path over there.'

They continued along the path in silence. Selma spotted a few groups of people in the distance. *That had to be the dividing line.* 'There.' Selma pointed to the gathering crowd.

'Yes, I see. I hope they are both alive and well.'

Selma bit her lip as reality crashed back; her son and husband had been captured by the enemy. Her heart hammered in her chest; they were both a fundamental part of her. She needed them to live.

Selma and Kemal finally reached the piece of land that divided Muslim from Serb. There was a crowd on both sides of that line, and it was clear who belonged to which side. The Muslim soldiers were in uniforms, the design of which seemed to be put together at the last minute – the blue and yellow emblem with two crossed swords and lilies emblazoned on their arms.

The Serbian prisoners standing behind the soldiers did not look good. Their skin was sallow, and their large eyes were filled with fear and confusion. Selma did not dare look at the Serbian prisoners too much. She averted her eyes as soon as one of them looked at her. She put her head down. She and Kemal were told to stand with a group of about fifty people waiting for their family members. There were about twenty-five Serb prisoners waiting to be exchanged.

Then a group of Muslim prisoners were approaching on the other side and she searched the faces for her son and husband.

Then a woman from her group shouted excitedly: 'There he is, there! Yes, it is him. Of course it is him.' Then she yelled 'Samir, Samir! Look at me, it's your mother.'

Others pulled the yelling woman back into the crowd. 'Calm down woman! Be quiet. Do you want to stop this exchange altogether?'

Selma kept scanning the approaching prisoners surrounded by Serbian soldiers. It had been four months since she had last seen them; they could not have changed that much.

Her eyes flicked over the prisoners again and again as her heart pounded. They were still too far away to recognise. When she turned to Kemal he was ashen, but Selma was too preoccupied with her own worry to try and comfort her father-in-law.

'Will they read their names out?' she asked, finding some common territory with her father-in-law.

'How else would they do the exchange?' Kemal's expression did not change. He was not mocking Selma; it was a comforting exchange of words between them, soothing.

'Can you see either of them?'

Kemal shook his head while persistently scanning the group of prisoners. 'There he is! That is him! I am sure.' Kemal turned to Selma, still trying to keep quiet. 'Look behind that man with white beard, in a blue shirt. See?'

Selma raised herself on her toes, swaying from side to side to get a clear view. 'Yes, I see! My son. My son.' She put her hand to her mouth as her eyes welled with tears. Kemal gave her a hug of encouragement. 'But where is my husband? Why are they not together?'

'He must be somewhere in the group. We just cannot see him.'

Selma started waving at her son. A few prisoners were waving, too. Though they were waving at their loved ones, Selma smiled at them, needing to share this moment with as many people as possible.

Selma accosted an older looking woman, her head covered in scarf. 'Who have you come to meet?'

The woman gazed at Selma. 'My husband. I recognised him in the crowd.'

'Oh, great. I am meeting my son. Yes, yes I saw him, too. I cannot see my husband, though,' Selma said with slight fear and then continued. 'I don't know why. I am sure he is there. Oh, my son! Oh, this wretched war! But, I guess they know what they are doing.' Selma turned to Kemal, and he made a face as if to say: *"Stop that blubbering, woman."*

So, Selma smiled at the woman she spoke with and kept gazing at the group, trying to get her son's attention. Then she heard somebody say: 'Here, they are starting now. Quiet!'

There was no ceremony. There were no red roses, no red carpet, but though elation filled the air, it was tempered by screams or quiet crying of those whose loved ones were not returning.

Names were being called: a Serbian name from one side; a Muslim name from the other. When her son's name was read out, Selma froze. Kemal grabbed her by the arm and pulled her towards the dividing line.

'That's our boy.' Kemal's voice was strong.

When Haris approached, she pulled him into a fierce hug and kissed him all over his face. He smelled musty, of the earth, of sleeping rough in barns, but she kissed all that – her son was home.

Kemal grabbed him and held him close, the hug saying more than words ever could.

'Where is your father?' Selma asked. 'Is he with you?'

Haris' haggard face and solemn eyes looked first to Selma then his grandfather; guilt darkened his expression. 'I don't know,' Haris said. 'I lost touch with him, two days ago. We were together the whole time, but when I woke yesterday morning he was gone. I don't know. I don't. I don't know.'

Kemal pulled his grandson to his chest. 'Don't think of that now. Everything will be fine.' Then he turned to Selma. 'Selma, you two wait here for me.'

Selma looked on as her father-in-law strode to one of the men holding what she guessed was a prisoner list. The man looked down at his notebook, running a finger down the page, before shaking his head. He pointed to another man a little away who also held papers and who also stood with some more lists in his hands.

As Kemal walked to that man, Selma turned to her son forcing a smile: 'What do you want to eat when we get home? Are you hungry?'

'Mum, all you think about is feeding me. I am not hungry. I am tired and just want to sleep in a clean bed.'

'I know dear, I know. I wish I could have taken your place.' Selma held his face in her hands.

'Now don't cry, Mum, please. I am safe.'

Kemal returned, his face flushed. 'They don't know where Seid is.' Kemal glanced at Selma and Haris with despair in his eyes. 'Apparently, Serbs are saying, that some of them tried to escape, so ...' Kemal stopped for a moment, catching a breath. 'We will have to leave without him and I gave those men...' Kemal pointed, 'our details, and they will contact us. Let's go.'

Selma shook her head. 'I don't want to go without my husband!'

Kemal gave her a stern look. 'Selma, we have no option. It is not what you or I want, but we have to leave without him.'

Selma started shaking violently. 'I want my husband! I am not leaving without him.'

Kemal's face darkened; his brows drew together in anger, he gripped her arms. 'Now listen. I don't want to leave without my son. Do you understand? But I have no choice. I can scream and shout, but nobody can help. I will just look like a fool. Now be quiet and let's leave.' He turned to his grandson: 'Hold on to your mother and let's go.'

Selma's lips trembled and she fought back tears as she grabbed onto her son: 'You are everything that I have.'

Melbourne, Australia, 2000s

Tanya woke quite early but stayed in bed thinking of the SMS message from Goran. He was back and he wanted to see her. She stretched in pleasure; her life had meaning.

Milica started meowing. Tanya got up and searched the cupboard delighted to find another can for Milica. *Need to get some cat food.* Milica happily scoffed the contents of her bowl and went to the front door. Tanya let her out then made a coffee before putting on a load of washing. As she ate she made a mental list of things to be done before going out that evening: shopping, vacuum, dust...

Tanya examined herself in the full length mirror. *My nose is a bit too wide. And my smile is not the best, but if I don't smile too wide – like so – yeah, that's not too bad.*

Dark-brown, shoulder-length hair framed her face, and her figure was quite slim, although she wondered how much longer it would stay slim. Right now, her age did not bother her as much as it normally did, and she guessed that was due to Goran.

She sighed; it was time to go shopping.

The day had gone fast, and it was time to get ready for her date with Goran. She dressed and applied makeup carefully, but when she looked in the mirror, she wasn't impressed. Two changes of clothes later she was ready to go. As she headed towards the door, she looked at the watch. It was quarter to five. Panic hit her. She was going to be late.

Goran was already waiting and he rose when she approached and kissed her gently on the lips; it was very natural. There would be no awkward moments between them. They chatted as if they had known each other forever and time passed quickly.

'Let's go to another café and have something to drink.' Goran led the way.

Having been in Melbourne longer than her, he knew all the places. He was as beautiful as a picture: striking smile, lovely jet-black hair he wore to his shoulders. It suited him. He was very fashionable. Just the way Tanya liked guys. He'd been married before, but had no kids. He told her a lot about his life in those few hours, but, even had he not, Tanya felt she understood him. *He is the one.*

As they got more amorous, he suddenly said. 'I would like to stay at your place tonight.'

Tanya's desire was there, but she wanted to take things little slowly. 'That's bit too soon, Goran.'

'Come on, we aren't kids. We don't have to do anything you don't want to,' he said with a cheeky smile.

Wait, she thought to herself. *Why not?* She wanted to be with him, and there was no thought for tomorrow, just for now, for this moment. Pure desire throbbed through her, but her practical side reared its head. 'No. Let's just meet again.'

Goran shrugged, and made a grimace of disappointment. 'Okay,' he said. 'Then kiss.'

The beep of a text message woke her and she reached for the mobile next to her bed. "Miss you" it read. She quickly wrote back "Miss you too" then looked at the time: 6am. *What is he doing up at this time?*

Her mobile phone rang; a private number. Confused, she answered: 'Hello?'

'Hi. Did you sleep well?'

'Goran, yes.' She smiled at the sound of his voice. 'I slept well but not very long. I am still in bed. Where are you?'

'I'm on cloud nine. Would you like to come up?'

She liked his flirting, it felt right. He was light and airy – she needed him, needed his fun and carefree ways. He helped her forget her worries.

She did not think about whether she loved him; she just went along. Isn't that what a woman was supposed to do? Follow her man? He was only working casually, but was hoping for a big job to come through, something to do with opening a shop.

Tanya's work at the agency was more and more on the wane and she started looking for a permanent work, but she was wrapped up in Goran.

Things seemed to move fast in Goran's life. In the span of a couple of weeks his business with a shop fell through, and he was now looking for a job. They grew closer and he visited Tanya at her place a few times. On Saturday afternoon a couple of months into their relationship he called.

'How was work today?' Goran asked Tanya.

'Okay. How about you? Did you get that interview?'

'Which interview? Oh, that one. Nah. I did call, but they told me that position was filled already.'

'Why did they advertise then?'

'I'm coming over your way today,' he said. 'How about if I pass by your place? Would you be at home?'

'Sure. What time would you be looking at coming over?' Tanya asked.

'Later in the afternoon.'

'Okay. Shall I make something for lunch?'

'No, I'll swing by Hungry Jacks on the way. Shall I bring you something?'

'No, thanks,' she said. 'You know I don't like fast food.'

'You are difficult sometimes.' Goran sounded annoyed.

'I am not,' Tanya said defensively.

'Just kidding. I know you cook better, but I don't want you to stress yourself. I'll eat out and—'

'But it is not stress—'

'I'll see you later. Cheerio.'

The line went dead.

At around four that afternoon Tanya answered the door.

'Hi,' Goran smiled, kissing her softly as he walked past.

'You smell of hamburger,' she told him.

'Well, I offered to get you one. At least I don't smell of another woman.' He grabbed her and kissed her again. 'Want some more hamburger?' He laughed, let her go, then went to sit on the couch.

'What's up?' she asked. 'What have you been doing? Do you want to go to the cinema? There's a good film I want to see—'

'Hold up,' Goran laughed. 'One question at a time.' He sighed. 'I'm tired. I don't feel like going anywhere.'

'Why don't you ever introduce me to your friends?' she asked.

Goran laughed again. 'What's with you? I'm not exactly a social butterfly, Tanya. You are far more intellectual than anybody I know. You'd be bored with the few people I know.'

Tanya didn't know what to say to that.

Goran looked at her. 'Tanya, you have far more than what I have. I don't have a job; I have very few friends. I can't offer you much.'

'I know. That's fine. I am not asking for more than what you are giving me.' Tanya smiled then tried to lean on him, but he stood and grabbed the remote control. 'What's on the telly?' he said and slumped back on the couch.

Tanya went to the kitchen to make coffee.

CHAPTER V

London, UK, 1990s

On Saturday morning, Celine went shopping. She walked into some small boutiques hoping to find something exquisite, and on one of the racks discovered a beautiful lime-green dress. She put it against her and studied herself in the mirror.

'That would suit you very nicely, Miss.'

Celine turned, surprised at the appearance of the sales assistant.

'If you do not mind me saying so,' the assistant added quickly. 'Would you prefer if I called you Madam?'

'Miss is fine,' Celine said. 'It does look nice, doesn't it?'

'Would you like to try it on? Our fitting room is at the back of the store.'

'How much is it? Two hundred and fifty pounds. Hmm... I'll try it on.'

Celine went to the fitting room and closed the curtain. As she slipped the dress on, it made her feel like Cinderella the night she met her prince. *God, will this be the dress?*

She left the fitting room to look at herself in the full-length mirror. The pencil-skirt hem sat just across her knees and was figure-hugging, accentuating her bottom perfectly. The top part of the dress had a scoop collar and sat elegantly on her shoulders. The dress made her green eyes seem greener, and her black curls flowed over her shoulders. *Mark will love it.*

'It definitely suits,' said the sales assistant. 'It really looks beautiful.'

Celine agreed, and bought the dress before continuing with her shopping, but she also needed to go and see Gina. She found a telephone booth and rang Ian. 'Hi Ian. It's Celine. Listen, the only time I could go and see Gina would be this afternoon. Give me the address of the hospital and I'll go talk to her.'

'Celine, you don't have to go and see her. It is just that—'

'Okay, okay. Just give me the address and I'll get there. I do need to talk to her. I understand Gina better, I can talk to her about things you cannot. Things that can only be said between girls.'

'Exactly. And—'

'But, I am just fucking tired of Gina and her fucking issues. Who is she to me to have to look after her?'

'Celine... she's our friend.'

'Yeah, whatever. I'll let you know how I go. Bye'

Celine continued window-shopping, slightly annoyed at having to stop in order to see Gina and talk to her about her pathetic life. As much as she wanted to go to her apartment and drop off her shopping, it was already three o'clock, so she had no choice but to go to the hospital from here.

When Celine entered the hospital room, Gina was lying on a bed. 'Hi Gina.'

'Hey, hello Celine. I didn't expect you.' Gina seemed genuinely surprised to see Celine.

Celine was about to say that Ian had asked her to come and see Gina, but she stopped herself. 'Well, as the English say: a friend in need is a friend indeed.'

Gina turned her face away, but not before Celine saw sadness settle in the woman's eyes. 'How are you feeling?' Celine said softly. 'Is this where you want to be?'

Gina snapped her head around, her eyes narrowed. 'Why would I want to be here?' Gina stared at Celine, her head twitching, her fingers tapping on the side of the bed.

Celine put her shopping down, then held the back of the chair next to the Gina's bed. 'Sorry, Gina I did not express myself well.' She let go of the chair, and stood at the foot of the bed. She glanced around the room. 'Do you think a place like this will be helpful to you? Would it help you resolve some of your issues?'

'What issues?'

'Well, for starters... you look depressed. You need rest.' Celine walked to the window, turned around and leaned on the sill. 'You need to discuss all this with a psychologist or a psychiatrist. One-on-one. Slowly. Explain all that bothers you. Try and get an understanding of why everything has come to this.' She walked to Gina's bed and sat in the chair. 'Try and focus. Where do you want to go in life? If I were down I would find that a place like this would be perfect for me to gather my thoughts and clear my head of everything that was clogging it up and stopping me from moving on.'

'That is all very well said.' Gina seemed pensive for a moment, almost lost in her own world as she stroked her chin. 'But you do understand that I am going to be moved to a ward. Like, full on.' Gina had fire in her eyes. 'There will be people with all kinds of mental illness around me.'

'Ignore it. Just concentrate on what you need,' Celine said as she leaned towards Gina.

'True. I'll try,' Gina said softly.

Celine glanced her watch and then carefully studied Gina. She moved over to Gina's bed. 'Here,' she said, and embraced Gina.

'You smell nice,' Gina muttered.

Celine released Gina, walked to her bag and fished something out of it. 'Here,' she gave Gina a bottle of perfume. 'I've gone off that scent anyway.'

Gina took the bottle and turned it over in her hands. 'Thanks,' she whispered.Celine grabbed her bags. 'That's okay. Now try and get some rest and remember what we said is important while you're here.'

Celine walked out of the hospital feeling very positive. She ran across the road and away from that nasty place. She knew Ian was right. Gina was their friend, a crazy friend, but a friend nevertheless.

It was well past eight o'clock when Celine got home. She checked her messages and made a mental note to call her English friend first thing the next morning and nonchalantly mention her business trip to Vienna. As Celine headed to the kitchen the second message started playing. Mark. She returned to the machine and rewound the message. 'Hi Celine. Please give me a call when you come back. There's a slight change of plans. Nothing serious. Just some airport arrangement changes. Bye for now.'

Should I call him immediately? Should I wait? Why should I wait? He does not know what time I got home. I'll call him. Celine looked at the clock – eight-thirty. He might think her some sad creature that had nowhere to go on Saturday night. She thought for a moment longer and then dialled the number.

Mark's deep voice answered. 'Hello.'

'Hi, Mark, it is Celine. I just got home, but am about to head out again. What is happening with the transport tomorrow?'

'Oh, yes, sure. It's nothing major. I'll be taking a taxi to the airport, so if you'd like, I'll come by your place to pick you up on the way, if that's okay?'

'Is there a problem?' Celine asked, but there was no reply from his side, she quickly moved on. 'What time were you planning to pick me up?'

'The flight's at six, so I guess about three in the afternoon?' Mark seemed a little unsure, but Celine would be strong.

'Three sounds good.'

'Yes, three pm, that's the plan,' Mark confirmed.

'Excellent, see you tomorrow at three then. I am so looking forward to this,' she said, sending all her positive energy down the telephone line.

'Well, it's going to be hard work,' Mark said, sounding a bit confused.

'Mark, I always wanted to be part of a project like this. I will do my best to make it easier on you, and I will actually enjoy doing it.'

'Thanks Celine. You're a gem.'

Celine put the phone down and clutched her hands together. *I cannot wait to get my hands on him.*

Mark put the phone down and turned around to see Kate standing behind him. 'What's the matter, sweetheart?' Mark said putting his hand on Kate's shoulder and gazing intently into her eyes.

'I really don't want you to go,' Kate said in low voice.

'Kate, my love, I am going for work, that's all.' Mark put his arms around her and held her for a moment, before Kate broke away gently.

'I just have a bad feeling about all this,' Kate said, looking away.

Mark roared with laughter. 'You do make me laugh sometimes. Where do you get that bad feeling from? Come to the sitting room, come on, we'll talk.' Mark frowned as he led Kate to the sofa and sat her down, settling himself beside her. 'Kate, you're pregnant. You need to be relaxed. You mustn't get all worked up about my trip and you need to understand I'll have lots of trips like this.'

'I know, I know, but I'm quite emotional, and I expect you to be here with me when I am in this state. And Mark, we're not even married yet.'

'Well all of this came as a bit of a surprise, Kate.'

'What came as a surprise? My pregnancy?' Shock widened her eyes.

'Well, you have to admit we didn't exactly plan it.'

'Mark!' Kate leapt to her feet, anger etched on her features. 'I did not plan this!'

Mark remained seated while Kate stood there with tears in her eyes, obviously expecting him to say something. But all he could do was sit there helplessly. Kate stomped from the room. 'Kate, I have my job to do,' he yelled after her.

Mark went to the bar and poured himself a good measure of whiskey before sitting at the window and staring into the garden. It was important he be focused on his job; he needed to get this office in Vienna up and running especially now he had a baby on the way. He needed to concentrate on getting his family safe and secure, but at the back of his mind was that nagging feeling he'd been thrown into something for which he was not ready.

Celine woke elated. Mark would be picking her up so it was time to get organised and packing. She put her new dress against her body and looked in the mirror; she would organise an evening out with Mark where she would wear this.

When the intercom rang at three in the afternoon, she looked around her apartment to make sure she had not forgotten anything, then locked the door behind her, dragging her heavy luggage down the stairs.

'My God,' Mark said when he saw her. 'That's a lot of luggage for a couple of weeks.'

Celine gave Mark a big smile and she stood impatiently at the boot of the car looking intolerantly at the driver. 'Sorry, Madam,' the driver said as he popped the boot and loaded the luggage.

As Celine sat at the back of the taxi with Mark, she felt like she was with her Prince Charming. The drive was uneventful except for a moment when Mark reached across her and popped the security button on the door, accidentally brushing his arm against Celine's chest. Celine only had to lean slightly forward to make this happen. She looked at him with a slight embarrassed smile, and her cheeks blushed on command. Mark excused himself but his cheeks remained red for a moment and he kept silent for the remainder of the trip. After few attempts to chat him up during the trip to the airport, Celine gave up as Mark seemed entrenched in his thoughts.

Mark let her have a choice of seat, so she took the one next to the window. He smiled as he took his seat. 'Are you scared?'

Celine laughed softly. 'I'm fine. Really. I have travelled by plane quite a few times.' Celine felt something was worrying Mark. 'Are you okay?' she asked.

'I'm fine.'

'Maybe, you are worried about this project? It is a lot of work on your shoulders. You know that I will do my best to help you out.'

'No, I'm not too worried about the job. We're meeting someone from the previous business when we arrive.'

'Are we going to keep the majority of people from that company?'

'That's a good question, but would they be willing to work for us? And would they want to change to our way of doing the business? I don't know. That's something we need to work on. You can speak German, can't you?'

'Yes, I can.'

'Excellent.'

Celine was still not happy that she hadn't gotten to the bottom of what was worrying him, so she pushed on. 'How did Kate take that you would be apart for the next few weeks?' Celine immediately regretted the question as Mark looked at her with almost hatred in his gaze. Celine held his gaze managing to feign indifference but Mark leaned back, closing his eyes and ignoring her question.

When they arrived in Vienna they hired a car, Mark handing Celine a map of the city. 'Could you just hold this in case we get lost?' he said as they settled in the car.

'Not a problem.' Celine was happy to act as an assistant and just enjoy looking at the scenery as Mark drove to their hotel. Night was slowly falling on the scattered houses and paddocks on the side of the road. As they approached Vienna, houses grew closer to each other until they finally found the road that was to take them to the hotel.

They were given two separate double rooms next to each other. 'I'll go and freshen up and then perhaps we could go for a drink in the town?' Mark suggested.

'Sounds good,' Celine said, and retreated to her room. When she returned to the lobby, she found Mark with a drink in his hand. 'You started without me?'

'Did you want a drink here?'

'No, I'd rather have one in town.'

They were close to the centre of the town, so it was a nice walk. As they found a café Mark quickly ordered a drink, which he downed even more quickly before looking for a waiter to order another.

There was not much conversation between them, so Celine tried to seize the moment. 'You are enjoying having a drink tonight?'

Mark did not answer, so she waited until he had downed a few more drinks before starting again. 'I am enjoying it here, I feel free, and Vienna is lovely, isn't it?'

'It is,' Mark finally said.

Celine felt the door was opened. 'You do look a little tense. I hope you're not too worried about this job. We'll make it work and I'll be with you every step of the way.' Mark held her gaze and she put her hand over his. 'You know that, don't you? You know that I'll support you.'

She thought she saw tear in his eye. She slid her hand up his arm, and he had a puzzled look for a moment then it changed into something more intense. She moved closer and held him, and his arms moved around her. Celine moved her lips closer to his cheek.

Mark turned his head, his lips brushing over hers. 'Let's go back to the room,' he said. 'This is mad, Celine.'

'I know, but it is good madness.' Celine was totally in control, as she knew she had to be.

Lying beside him she ran her fingers over his chest and stomach, and as he looked at her, she thought he was caught in that moment. She turned to her stomach and lifted her head to be closer to him. 'I hope you will not regret this in the morning?'

'Maybe slightly,' he said and smiled cheekily.

Celine pretended to slap him and laughed too.

'What's the time?'

Celine turned to her night cabinet and fumbled for her watch. 'Quarter past eleven.'

Mark started to get up. 'I'll go back to my room.'

Celine's heart sank but she feigned cool again 'You can stay here.'

'Thanks but it won't look right, us coming out of the same room in the morning.' He got out of bed and dressed quickly. He leant down and kissed her. 'It's good that our rooms are so close,' he said, smiling as he reached the door.

'You cheeky little monkey!' Celine called out before he closed the door.

Now, the battle begins. Hold on to your seats, we are taking off. Can I handle this well? Thousands of thoughts raced through her head and rivers of emotion flooded her body. *I have to sleep and be professional tomorrow. I have to impress him with being able to handle all this like a big girl. I am going to be the person he does not even know he wants and needs.*

Celine joined Mark the next morning for breakfast. 'Morning, did you sleep well?' said Celine as she approached the table with her breakfast.

Mark was all smiles. 'Yes, perfect.' Mark settled back into his chair and carried on eating his food.

'What time do we need to be at the office?' she asked.

'You forgot already,' he said with a grin. 'Half past eight will be fine.' Mark bit into croissant then took a sip of coffee.

'Do you know how to get there?' Celine was swirling spoon around her bowl of muesli as she glanced around the restaurant.

'Yes, I'll drive. Have you brushed up on your German?'

'Sure, I had plenty of time after you left my room.' Celine wanted some sort of reaction from Mark regarding last night.

'Was I in your room last night?' he asked, acting surprised.

'Yep, I got you drunk and seduced you.'

'All you foreign girls are like that. Use us poor British boys.'

'Mark, I like you.'

Mark looked at her slightly puzzled. 'I like you, too.'

'I don't want to make this trip look frivolous, I am aware that we have a job to do but I did not plan last night.'

'I never said you did.'

'I want more,' she said.

Mark pushed back in his chair, as though trying to put distance between them. 'What do you mean you want more?' A dark cloud came over his face.

'I mean, I like you,' said Celine, trying to save the situation, 'and I would like you to think the same way of me.'

'I do like you.' Mark's eyes glazed over; *was he thinking of that woman back home?*

Celine decided it would be wise to leave it at that, at this stage, and asked instead. 'Am I dressed correctly for today's meeting?'

'You're dressed fine,' said Mark somewhat distracted.

'Everything will be good, you will see,' Celine told him.

'What will be good?' Mark seemed to be growing more suspicious and that was the last thing Celine wanted.

'Today's meeting,' Celine explained. 'This whole project in Vienna, it will be good.'

'Sure.'

Celine struggled to concentrate at the office but forced herself to focus on the task at hand, making sure she was available and helpful to Mark whenever he needed her. As they were driving back to the hotel he congratulated her for her efforts and while she was delighted, she just gave him a very humble nod and thanked him.

Mark did not want to have dinner but wanted to go back to his room for an early night. Celine nodded her understanding, telling him she would have a drink at the bar before going to bed.

As she was sitting at the bar and having her drink, she was trembling. She kept glancing at the lift and stairs hoping Mark would come and join her for a drink. If he didn't she knew it was not the end of the world but if he did it would strengthen the connection between them. Just as she was finishing her drink the lift door opened and she glanced at it and struggled not to show too much enthusiasm.

'Well, one drink won't do me much harm,' Mark said with a boyish grin as he approached her. 'Would you have another one?'

'So, what made you change your mind?'

Mark frowned lightly. 'I don't know, I guess I don't like to be on my own.' He turned, leaning his elbows on the bar 'It's a fine hotel, isn't it?'

'It sure is. It looks very classy although it is not that expensive,' Celine said.

The rest of the conversation flowed nicely and Celine was pleased she had changed into a tight-fitting dress. She was flirting lightly as she did not want to scare him off. She knew she had to be available in measures and yet keep it uncertain. Mark had one more drink before Celine suggested she was tired and wanted to go back to her room. They stood in the corridor for a short while, and Celine certainly did not want to push for anything serious to happen. She did, however, put her arm around his shoulder, and then slid her hand to the back of his neck as she kissed him on the corner of the mouth. Mark looked at her wide-eyed as if he wanted to suggest something more, but Celine smiled and pushed the key into the keyhole before opening the door and disappearing behind it.

The next day was like a carbon-copy of the day before, except that Celine felt slightly more empowered. She learned the routine. She was not going to allow herself to make a wrong move. She was as helpful to Mark as she could be. She was the picture of a perfect assistant. Every now and then she would look at his fine profile and had wanted to grab him and take him with her. His suits were impeccable. Today he was in a grey, thinly-striped suit with pink shirt that perfectly complemented his chiselled jaw and ash blond hair and blue eyes. His shoes were just slightly pointed and polished to a high shine. Celine could not work out how he would get them to look so perfectly clean.

She had kissed him that evening before they went to their separate rooms. On the fourth night, he suggested they go out for a drink since it was Friday and they did not have to work early in the morning. Celine accepted. She went to the room and spent an hour getting ready. It was worth it, as when she went down to the bar to join Mark, she noticed few men at the bar looking at her, and he smiled feeling proud to be the one she would join.

She kissed him keeping her eyes on him only.

Celine felt on top of the world as she walked next to Mark. She knew he was not hers yet, but she certainly did not want to mention Kate... or whatever her name was. 'This is quite crazy, don't you think?'

'What is crazy?' Mark seemed genuinely confused.

'Us being together.'

'Are we together?'

'Yes, we are together in the street. Now. At this moment.' Celine did not want to stir trouble; she just needed some kind of confirmation.

'Well, I guess we are together. In the street. Now. At this moment.'

'Are you going to repeat everything I say from now on?' Celine asked playfully. She grabbed him by the arm and slid it down to his wrist, holding his hand in hers. Desire wove through her whole body, but she did not act on it. *Just a moment of weakness.* Instead, she looked him in the eyes. By the way Mark looked at her, she knew he felt the same. They went to a first bar and sat in a quiet corner. He leaned over and kissed her putting his hand on her bare leg. She felt totally powerless.

Mark felt a strong desire to have Celine. For a fleeting moment, Kate crossed his mind. *What she doesn't know won't hurt her. This is purely physical. Nothing to it. Besides I need this. And Celine is keen.*

'Can I sleep in your room tonight?' Mark whispered in Celine's ear as he dragged his lips across her cheek.

'We'll see how we go.'

'We are already gone, what are you talking about?' Celine laughed as Mark did and she playfully pushed him away. 'Have you noticed me in this way before?'

'When before?' Mark was again totally bewildered.

'In the office. Back in London.'

'Yes, I've noticed you. We work together. That's why I asked you to come with me to Vienna.'

'Yes, but did you ask me because you were hoping for something like this?'

Mark pulled back and took a swig from his bottle. 'I wasn't planning this if that's what you mean?'

Celine quickly regrouped. 'I did not say you planned this, but did you fancy me back in London, in the office?'

'I thought you were sexy. Yes.'

'I thought that about you, too.' Celine did not want to miss a beat.

'So you planned this?'

'Of course.' They both laughed. 'Just kidding. I need this type of experience for my future work, be it with Pluto or another publishing company.'

'Are you planning on leaving Pluto?'

'Not at all. Certainly not now. I want to be around you,' Celine said with a smile.

Mark pulled back again. 'You do understand that I have obligations back in London?'

'Obligations? Such as?' Celine asked innocently.

'I'm living with my girlfriend. Well, we still have separate apartments, but we're together.'

'Oh. Have you been with her for a while?'

'A few months... maybe a year.'

'Do you love her?' Celine's voice was so low it was barely a whisper.

'I don't know.' Mark took another swig from his beer bottle.

'I'll get you another drink.' Celine motioned to the waiter then turned to Mark and put her hand on his. 'It will all work out well, you will see.'

'I'm not so sure.' Mark looked like a small child and Celine leaned over and hugged him. Celine thought of the sadness of her own situation and her eyes glimmered. 'Everything will be all right. You will see,' she said again.

'Are you crying?' Mark asked.

'No, I am fine. I am just slightly confused about my feelings for you.' She looked at him for reaction. 'All I can promise you is that I will be with you every step of the way. Come hell or high water.'

'That's bit strong.'

'I love that way.' Celine put her hand on his arm and then lifted it to the nape of his neck and kissed him. Celine felt Mark pull away, so she turned the conversation back to work and once he relaxed they headed back to the hotel.

Mark stroked her hair gently and she looked at him with innocence. Her eyes welled up a bit, and she leaned over to him. He could feel her firm breasts pressed against his chest.

As they were walking back to the hotel, he didn't really want the night to end. 'Shall we have another drink at the bar?'

'Yes of course.' Celine felt that he wanted to be with her longer. She knew this was her moment. As they sat at the couch in one of the lounge areas, she felt relaxed. Mark decided to sit next to her.

'I do not want to leave Vienna,' Celine said.

'I know. It's lovely, isn't it? We've got two more weeks of this bliss.' And then he straightened. 'Well, and there is work to be done too.'

'Now that this publishing house in Vienna belongs to Pluto will you come here and work? Sort of, help them out. I don't know, guide them?'

'No. I don't really see the reason for that. They were publishing before. They know what they're doing. It's just matter of setting it under the Pluto banner and having things done the Pluto way. All of that can be controlled from London.' Celine made an upset face. 'What's that for?' he nudged her lightly. 'Oh, I see you wanted to come to Vienna and work here.'

'With you.' Celine leaned against him 'I really enjoy being with you.'

'I enjoy being with you too, but things aren't so simple.'

Celine felt her anger, but she quickly calmed herself. Anger would not help this situation. She needed patience. When he suggested going to her room that evening she made an excuse of being too tired. 'We'll go on a tour bus tomorrow, ok?' Celine tried to end on a high note.

'Sure, see you in the morning.' Mark was already leaving.

Back in her room, Celine was frantically thinking. *I don't like how this night ended. He is vulnerable now, and I need to be with him. Exactly!* Celine quickly picked her room keys, sprayed a bit more of her favourite Gucci perfume then went and knocked on Mark's door. There was an impatient 'Yes' from inside the room.

'Room service, Sir.' Celine tried to be relaxed.

Mark opened the door and Celine smiled covering her uncertainty as to his reaction to her change of mind. He pulled her in, stepped out looking left and right. 'Nobody followed you. That's good.' Celine hummed the theme from James Bond movie, and he grabbed her and while kissing her, walked her to the bed. Celine knew she had to be with him that night, and she would make sure he wouldn't forget a moment of it.

From then on, Celine felt a change of pace between them. It felt as if they were in a real relationship. She did everything not to spoil that: she never asked any untoward questions, she learned to read his expressions for answers that he needed, and react accordingly. *Slowly, slowly catch the monkey.* This phrase would make Celine smile, and when she would look at Mark, he would smile back.

The last night in Vienna was hard. Celine's stomach was knotted, and she could not even look at her suitcase. The flight was not till noon the next day, which was well planned, as the last night in Vienna had to be about going out with people from the office, and the leaving party dinner with them.

'I don't feel like spending the evening with them. I want to be with you.' Celine felt free to vent her frustration.

'We'll have a drink, something small to eat and then we'll leave. Okay?'

Celine did not have any choice. That was the best thing to do.

'Actually, it was not too bad,' Celine said as they were leaving the restaurant.

'Do you want to go back?' Mark was almost serious.

'It wasn't that good. We said our goodbyes and I think it was the right time to leave anyway.'

'Let's go for a proper drink somewhere now.'

They sat at one of the outside tables and ordered drinks. They were both watching beyond the passers-by.

'What are you thinking about?' Celine was eager to keep the connection going.

'Nothing special.'

'I want us to stay in touch in London.' Celine looked at Mark for any signs of where things were heading.

'We'll stay in touch. We work together.' Mark was still a bit distant.

Celine did not want to push too hard. Her stomach was knotted again, and frustration was rising inside of her. 'Let's go back to the hotel.' And the moment she said it, she regretted it.

Mark took a big swig from his bottle and said, 'Let me just pay for this.'

They were both very quiet as they walked to the hotel and as they walked to her room, Celine was not sure what to do. She turned to him and kissed him lightly.

'Good night.'

'Good night, Celine. Sleep tight.'

The next morning, Mark found Celine at the restaurant. He waved at her then went to the buffet before joining her. He leaned across the table and kissed her. 'Why the sunglasses?'

'I did not sleep well.' Celine was not looking for sympathy, she was just telling the truth. 'My eyes are all puffed up, and, I guess, it is better to cover it up.'

'I didn't sleep well either. It's the change of routine. And the travel.'

Celine could not help but think. *Why did he not want to be with me last night? He is actually worried and unsure, just like me.* Celine then looked at Mark with a look of approval, although she realised that he could not see that. Still, that thought made her feel better. 'I'll miss Vienna. Maybe one day we will come back here again. Not for a business trip just for fun.' Celine felt light and relaxed with that thought.

'That's a deal.' Seemed Mark was in a good mood too.

Celine woke to a cold autumn morning. The weather had changed quickly from the previous week; the short, warm British summer had gone straight into a cold, windy autumn with leaves turning amber seemingly overnight.

Mark was distant and Celine felt nervous with the whole situation, but she was not going to give up. At times, his reserved demeanour made her feel like she should just throw in a towel, but pride and anger would well up in her – she would not let him go so easily.

He was constantly on her mind and the rest of her life was barely holding together. She was constantly around him at work and she tried to make her calls and visits to his office meaningful. It did not seem like he was avoiding her, more that his mind seemed to be elsewhere.

They were alone in his office when she said: 'I miss Vienna.' Celine rarely mentioned Vienna but she felt that it was time to use every available weapon in her arsenal.

Mark looked at her and sighed. 'You do?'

'I think of you all the time.' She came closer to his desk. 'Mark, why couldn't we have a drink one night?'

'Celine, you knew very well that I was with someone.' He gave her a sad smile. 'I know it just happened. I mean, I do like you, and I think of you too, but I can't.'

'Mark, there is no harm in a drink.' Celine was holding all her frustration in check as she smiled.

'Okay, let's have a drink.'

'This week?' Celine knew that Kate was away that week 'This Friday? Tomorrow?'

He frowned then smiled. 'Okay, yes. Let's have a drink tomorrow.'

'I like you Mark.'

He looked at her, but there seemed to be pain etched on his face, 'I like you too, Celine.'

'I like so many things about you, Mark.'

His face lit up. 'I like many things about you, too.'

'Well then, I am looking forward to tomorrow.' Celine made a swirl towards the door, then turned and smiled at him and left the office.

Mark watched Celine leave. *I like that gentle sway of her hips. And she's so eager. She doesn't give me a hard time, just pure pleasure. Kate doesn't have to know. Celine doesn't know her and wouldn't tell her anyway. Besides, it's been ages since I've had any fun. Life is far too short to worry about little things like this. I'll have a lifetime to be settled down when Kate has the baby, and things become too serious for this kind of fun.* Mark smiled to himself and looked over to Celine's booth where she was watching him.

They met at a restaurant where waiters already thought they were a couple. *I must make sure not to bring Kate here.*

'Did you miss me today?' Celine flirted.

'Of course I missed you. I've missed you since Vienna,' he told her.

'But you have not done anything about that.' Celine tried to make a serious face.

'You could have done something too,' Mark said with a smile.

When Celine touched Mark's hand he saw desire in her eyes. 'What do you think if we skip dinner?'

'We are far from my place,' Celine said.

'Let's go to a hotel.' Mark was decisive.

'No, that is tacky.' Celine pouted. 'Don't you live close to here?'

'We can't go to my place.'

'Why not?'

'Because I don't live by myself.' Mark's doubt resurfaced, but... 'Mind you, at the moment I'm alone.'

Celine wanted to say 'I know' but instead said 'Well let's go to your place then. I would like to see it.'

They started kissing in the car in front of Mark's building. 'Now, control yourself young lady... till we get in.' Mark opened the car door, and they went to the building quickly. Mark pulled her into the apartment. 'Don't just stand there,' he said, then kissed her as he closed the door behind her. 'Do you want a drink?'

'Do you?'

'No, not really.' He kissed her again and nudged her towards the bedroom door.

Celine relinquished all her power over as her half naked body touched the bed sheets. Their lovemaking was more passionate than she ever experienced in Vienna.

When it was over he lay staring at the ceiling then got up and went to the bathroom. Celine looked around the room: built-in robes, side table with alarm clock and a book. She got out of bed and went to the wardrobe; there were some women's clothes but some of Mark's too. Celine took one of her earrings and dropped it on the wardrobe floor then pushed it under Kate's clothes then took out her other earring and dropped it into her bag. She then studied herself in the full length mirror, pleased with what she saw.

When Mark returned, wearing his briefs, Celine demurely pulled the sheet off the bed and wrapped it around herself.

'You have a gorgeous body, Celine,' he said removing the sheet. 'I can't get enough of it.' He kissed her pushing her back onto the bed.

'I love you, Mark.'

Mark grabbed her thigh. 'I love you too, Celine,' he said with a grunt.

'I don't want to leave. I want to stay with you.' Celine released herself and stretched her body alluringly fully aware that he was watching her with desire.

'I don't want you to leave either.' Mark lay on top of her and made love to her slowly as if to devour her thoroughly.

Mark looked very tired afterwards, and Celine felt it was the right time to push a little more. 'Does Kate live here?'

A cloud came over Mark's face 'She's here most of the time. Why are you asking?'

'It's just...' Celine shrugged. 'It is just that I would like to be here most of the time.'

Mark's expression softened. 'But you can't. You know that.'

'Yes, I do.' Celine was genuinely sad. 'Are we going to see each other more often?'

'We'll see each other in the office all the time,' Mark said gently, his fingers brushing down her face.

'But you will not marry me.'

'Celine, what's wrong with you?' Mark said with exasperation. 'I am practically already married. You know that.'

'Do you love her?'

Mark's expression darkened. 'Celine, this is neither the time nor the place for me to talk about her. She's a fine woman.'

That remark hit Celine like a knife to the stomach, and she rolled onto her side and pulled her knees to her chest. 'That hurts.'

'What hurts?' Mark was oblivious as he stared at her. He stood suddenly and begun dressing while Celine remained in the foetal position. 'How will you get home tonight?' Mark asked as he headed toward the bedroom door.

Celine felt her body was made of lead as she pulled herself in sitting position. 'I thought you would drive me home so we could be together for a bit longer.'

'I have to work tomorrow, and so do you.' He studied her for a moment. 'I'll take you to the tube though. It's not too late. You can get tube home.'

'Okay,' Celine said her legs dangling over the side of the bed. 'Okay, Mark.' Celine bottled her anger tight.

Celine made sure she was always close to Mark when at the office. When they were alone in his office, she whispered. 'I miss you, Mark.'

Mark gave her a sad smile. 'I miss you, too.'

'That's nice.'

Mark cocked his head then laughed loud at her words.

Celine chuckled, happy to have made him laugh. 'When are we going to see each other again?' Celine tried to make it sound casual.

'I don't know, Celine. It's bit rough at the moment.'

Celine frowned. 'What do you mean rough?'

Mark shrugged as he shuffled papers on his desk. 'Kate is behaving very strangely.'

'Maybe it is a pregnancy thing.'

Mark shook his head in negation. 'She was pregnant befo—' He frowned as he looked to her. 'How do you know she's pregnant?'

'You've told me, I guess,' Celine said as casually as possible.

Mark's face turned red. 'You knew that and you slept with me?' He put his palms on the desk as he stared at Celine awaiting her answer.

Fury surged through Celine. 'Well, you knew and you still slept with me.'

They glared at each other for a brief moment then Mark changed the subject with a shrug. 'I don't know, Celine.' He sighed. 'Kate is distant and for some funny reason she keeps accusing me of having an affair?' Mark looked to Celine for help. 'You wouldn't have said anything?'

'Mark, I don't know Kate.'

He gave her a sheepish look. 'Of course. I'm sorry.'

'If there is anything I can do to help—' Celine started before Mark interrupted her.

'Thanks but no.' He gave her a warm smile. 'I know I can count on you.'

Celine leaned over and gently stroked his hand. 'And don't ever forget that Mark.' Celine then added reassuringly, 'I do have spare couch if you need it.'

'It might be coming to that,' Mark muttered.

Celine hid her delight and looked him straight in the eye. 'Mark, my door is always open for you.'

As Mark locked his gaze at her, Celine thought that he had never looked at her that way. As she went back to her desk and lifted her eyes in direction of his office she realised that he was still staring at her. She felt uncomfortable for a moment but then she returned the gaze, but this long stare they shared made her feel that something was changing in Mark's view of her, something was developing, although she could not tell if it was the beginning or the end.

Celine was not feeling at ease. Every now and then she would snap at anybody who made even the smallest remark; she was irritable and she knew that it was due to the frustration of the situation with Mark. She needed him but she also knew she had to be careful not to overburden him with any demands. She dressed and looked immaculate when at work, tried to be a more sophisticated lady, and Mark was paying attention.

He stared at her whenever she approached, but he never initiated contact. Celine decided it was time to act.

When she saw Mark alone in his office, she walked in and putting her palms on the desk leaned over. 'So, when are you finally going to come and see my place?'

Mark looked up at her, then down her v-neck and smiled at her. 'Whenever you invite me.'

Celine smiled. 'How come you are so easy?' Celine said with a smile.

'I like it easy.'

Celine raised an eyebrow. 'I thought you were almost married?'

'There's always divorce.'

'What about the baby?' Celine struggled to cover her shock.

'What baby? Celine, darling, I've got a job to do.'

'Sorry, Mark.' She turned to leave, then turned back. 'So, dinner, my place, tonight?'

Mark stretched his lips to reveal perfect teeth 'I guess we can have dinner as well.'

Celine blushed and left feeling delighted. When she sat at her desk, Mark was not looking this time.

Celine left work right on time, stopping to get groceries for dinner before heading home. It would be an easy dinner as she did not want to sweat in the kitchen; her appearance was far more important.

When she finally reached her small rented apartment her phone rang.

'Hello.'

'Hi, Celine, it's Ian. Can you talk? Or, have I called at the wrong time?'

'Ian, I am busy.' Celine sighed. 'I've got some friends coming over for dinner.'

'Oh, cool. I was just wondering how it all went with Gina?'

'Gina... Oh, yes it was fine. Listen can we talk over the weekend or maybe even next weekend would be better?'

'But Celine, I need to know if you—'

'Ian, I don't have time. I've got friends coming for dinner, and you know they don't like waiting. This is important for my job. I'll talk to you later, okay? Bye.'

Gina and her pathetic life. And Ian... I don't have time for that shit. I've got a life. Now, calm down. Mark is coming; that is all that matters. I wonder why he is behaving so strangely lately. I'll have to tread carefully this evening.

Celine put the food away before going to shower. The hot water seemed to wash her troubles away. She examined herself in the mirror, she liked watching her naked body. As she started putting makeup on the doorbell rang. She looked at the watch; *it could not be Mark*. She slipped on her bathrobe before looking through the spy-hole. `

'Mark, it is you?'

'Yes, are you going to leave me to wait out here?' he lowered his voice.

'I am in my bathrobe,' Celine whispered, and before waiting for his reply, opened the door.

'Hi.' Mark looked her up and down before closing the door behind him. He grabbed her around her waist and whispered in her ear 'I didn't come here for dinner, did I? We both know that.' He pressed his lips against hers. 'Now, where's your bedroom?' he mumbled as he quickly scanned the small apartment. Before waiting for an answer from Celine he pushed her towards the open door and onto a bed. He smiled as he looked at her naked body revealed by a slipped bathrobe. He took his sweater off in one move and joined her on bed.

Celine was lying on the bed, her hair still wet, her wet bathrobe scrunched at the foot of the bed.

'Shall we go out and have something to eat?' Mark asked.

'Don't you have any trust in my cooking?' Celine felt... used, but that was the price she had to pay.

'I do,' said Mark. 'I'm just hungry now.'

Celine rose from the bed and grabbed her bathrobe. 'I'll make something quickly.'

Celine made a couple of sandwiches, then took a bottle of wine from the fridge and grabbed two glasses. Juggling everything she walked back into her bedroom to see Mark lying silently on the bed and looking towards the window. 'You couldn't help me, could you?'

Mark jumped from the bed and took sandwiches and bottle from her. 'Don't you want to go to the table to eat?' Mark asked politely.

'The bed is bigger than my kitchen table,' Celine said with a laugh.

Mark opened the bottle and poured a glass of wine and handed it to Celine and she waited for him to pour a glass for himself before touching his glass with hers. 'I am so happy that you came this evening,' she said earnestly.

'I'm happy to be here.'

Celine wrapped her free arm around him and kissed his temple. 'I would really like if you would stay here with me tonight.'

Mark smiled. 'Of course.' He kissed her hair gently.

Celine could hardly sleep. Mark's heavy breathing was comforting but somewhat disconcerting, too. *What is going on with him? What is with Kate and the baby? I cannot ask any of these questions though. I just want him to stay with me, and hopefully all his baggage is not in the way.*

She felt Mark stir and turn towards her. She made love to him then he showered while she went to the kitchen and made coffee and a couple of pieces of toast, calling to Mark to come and have his breakfast. When he walked into the kitchen, he was dressed and they moved around and ate their breakfast like a young married couple.

Celine hardly uttered a word until she took a calculated risk in saying: 'Will you move in with me?'

Mark stared at her then turned to stare out the window. He finally went and drew a glass of water from the tap then returned to the table. 'I will.'

There was silence after that. Celine did not dare ask any other questions. This was enough for now.

'I have to go out now,' he said, 'but I'll come back this afternoon. What are your plans for the day?'

'Nothing special. I'll just potter around the place, might go out and do some shopping.'

'I'm meeting some friends for dinner this evening. Do you want to come with me?' Mark seemed really keen for Celine to go with him.

'Of course.' She smiled. 'Gladly.'

As soon as Mark left, Celine went back to bed to sleep.

She felt re-energised when she woke, and began pottering around the house, cleaning, dusting, doing the dishes. When she looked at her watch it was just after three in the afternoon, and she decided to call her friend Helen. She needed to share this joy with somebody.

'Hello.'

'Hi Helen. It's me, Celine. How are you?'

'Oh, hi Celine. I'm fine.'

Celine started with small talk. 'I have not heard from you in ages.'

'I was busy writing this new column. But, hey, heard you went to Vienna. Tell me all about it.'

'Oh, Helen, I completely forgot about Vienna. It was good.' Celine was so pleased that Helen connected that fact.

'Oh, c'mon. Did you go with Mark? And...'

'Well, something is cooking.'

'Get out of town! You and Mark. I cannot believe it. We must meet. You have to tell me all about it.'

Celine was beaming. 'I know. We'll have to have lunch one day. I'll give you a call.'

'Oh, the news, the little tiny, tiniest gossip. I love that.' And then as if she remembered. 'Hang on, didn't Mark have a relationship with some girl, Carol or something?'

Celine felt her blood run cold 'I don't know anything about that.'

'I'm quite sure something was going on there but, well, if he's with you, obviously. Oh, forget it. I'm just thinking aloud. Just give me a call and we'll have lunch. I have to go now. Love you, dear. Talk to you soon. Bye.'

Celine just managed to squeeze in her own farewell before the line went dead.

Mark returned about five pm and he brought a small suitcase with him. Celine hugged and kissed him before letting him unpack and relax. She was keeping her cool.

'Did you want something to eat?' Celine called out.

'No, we're having dinner this evening. Did you forget?'

'No, no. I just thought you might be hungry.'

There was no answer from Mark until several minutes later she heard him: 'Where could I hang my clothes?'

Celine panicked. 'I can make some space in this wardrobe with my clothes or there is another cupboard in the corridor.'

'I want to hang my clothes not a china collection. I don't need a cupboard. I'll hang my clothes here in your wardrobe, I didn't bring many anyway.'

'What time did you arrange for dinner?' Celine asked

'Seven o'clock. Is that okay?' Mark's response was bit edgy.

'I'll start getting ready.' Celine ignored his irritation. Once she was done with her beauty routine she started to dress. Mark was in the living room, but she couldn't hear him. 'When will you start getting ready?' Celine asked.

There was no answer, so she went to the living room looking for Mark. Mark was dozing on the couch. Celine just stood there for a moment and Mark opened his eyes. 'Were you sleeping?'

'No, I just had my eyes closed. I heard you earlier. What's the time?'

'Six o'clock.'

'God, we'll be late. We need to take the tube.'

They arrived at the small Italian restaurant on Piccadilly Circus at around seven. Mark waved to his friends across the restaurant as they were led to the table. Mark shook hands of two men and kissed their girlfriends on the cheek before introducing them to Celine.

Celine sat next to one of the girlfriends. She looked as if she walked out of the office with pin striped jacket on and white shirt. The woman quickly explained as if she knew what Celine was thinking: 'I'm in real estate,' she said, 'and I just had house inspection. What a gorgeous house it was. Worth every penny of its two million pounds.'

Celine choked a bit but went on feigning normality. 'I would pay even more if the place is right.'

The girlfriend looked at Celine and then turned to Mark. 'Well, lucky you.'

Celine felt bit uncomfortable figuring it was not the right thing to say.

'So, how did you and Mark meet?' Samantha, the real estate woman, asked.

'Uhmm,..' Celine expected this question, but not so soon. 'We work together.'

'He and Kate lived together, but it didn't mean much,' Samantha laughed softly. 'Obviously.'

Celine took a deep breath, looked around the table and realising the others had not heard anything, regained her composure and seized the moment. 'Why didn't it work?'

Samantha seemed to be taken aback for a short moment, but continued, 'Why didn't work? Why are you asking me that?'

'Why do you find it so strange that Mark and I fell in love because we work together, and have this strong connection between us?'

'True.' And then Samantha added ' Mark has been through some tough emotional times.'

What tough emotional times I wonder? Celine realised that these people knew far more about Mark than she did.

'I am sure Kate is a fine woman,' Celine said, 'but the chemistry between two people is hard to beat and I guess that is why Mark and I are together.'

'I understand, but Mark didn't take losing the baby so lightly.'

Celine pretended that she knew what the woman was talking about. 'It was not his decision to lose the baby.' Celine feigned knowing the situation.

'Well, it was not Kate's either!' the woman got slightly more heated before taking a calming breath. 'That's all in the past and I guess you're right, there's a great chemistry between you.'

'Thanks.' Celine appreciated that comment and considered this a win with his friends.

But Samantha just turned away from Celine and hardly spoke with her for the rest of the night. Celine felt slightly on the outer throughout the night but was happy just to be sitting amongst them.

She did not have anybody on the other side of her, and the only other person was Mark's friend across the table from her. They exchanged few words between them, and he seemed friendly enough. Celine learned that he was the boyfriend of the woman sitting next to him and that he worked in the finance industry.

Celine enjoyed the food which seemed exquisite, and she tried things she hadn't eaten before, but she did not let that show. There were some prawns in a lovely butter sauce and venison for main that she had splashed with three glasses of wine.

As they were leaving, Celine mentioned to the other girlfriend, Melisa, that it was a pity the two did not manage to exchange a word between them, but Melisa was not even trying to hide her disinterest. Celine remained nice regardless. Mark then took her arm, and they left the restaurant. When they were out on the street, he suggested they go to a nearby hotel.

'Why do you want to go to a hotel?'

'I kept looking at you all night, didn't you notice?' he grabbed her by the bottom.

'Mark, stop that. We are in the street.'

'Nobody knows you here. Don't you know that the chances of meeting the same person again in London are absolutely minimal?' He grabbed the nape of her neck and kissed her passionately while his other hand pulled her towards him. 'Do you feel what I feel?'

'Mark, you are drunk.'

'So what? I do get drunk. But right now let's get a room in the hotel.' He started pulling her by the arm towards the entrance of a hotel.

'Mark, why don't we go home and do it there?'

'Home. I don't have a home anymore. An empty home is not a home. And besides,' he looked her straight in the eyes. 'I don't really like your shabby little apartment.'

Celine felt her whole world spin, but those few glasses of wine, helped numb her pain. 'Well, if you want to go to the hotel, let's go then.' Celine felt overpowered but then... the hotel did look very posh.

CHAPTER VI

London, UK, 1990s

Ian called Carol feeling bit apprehensive as the last few days had been taken up with Gina and her issues. It was Saturday morning, and he was working the afternoon shift that day. Carol didn't answer so he left a short message, apologising for being unreachable and mentioning Gina and the relating problems. Although Carol was not exactly trying to reach him, Ian also added he would call her the following day.

He often asked himself why he was staying in relationship with Carol, but she was very easy to spend time with. She was fun and there were always some interesting people around her, and when they were together she seemed genuinely interested in him. She lit up the room whenever she entered. Carol was very vivacious and very different from those he was often surrounded by, such as Gina, who was sometimes too depressing – her dark moods would drag him down with her. Yet he felt strangely obligated. There wasn't anybody genuinely interested in her wellbeing, so it was somehow left to him.

Some of his other Serbian friends were quite gloomy and were a living day-to-day existence, which Ian knew was not going to get them far. Carol was bubbly, and she was quite gorgeous, a tiny frame topped with rust-coloured hair, gorgeous green eyes and a few freckles that gave her naïve, child-like looks.

Ian did not want to lose her although there was always a dark cloud hanging above them as if she was just about to walk out on him. His thoughts about Carol would always start with: why am I with her and why is she with me?

His doorbell rang, and he looked through the window of his second-floor bedsit down to the street to see who was ringing.

'Carol. What a surprise! Come up.'

'Hi hun. Buzz me in.'

When he opened the door and saw her standing there in her skinny jeans and her unironed shirt his heart begun to race. He hugged her and kissed her on the cheek.

'I missed you, sweetie pea.'

'Please don't call me sweetie pea,' she said. 'That is so dated.' Carol wrinkled her thin, freckled nose and tossed her hair.

'Sorry. Tell me the word I could call you with that is not dated,' Ian said closing the door behind her.

'We don't say 'word I could call you with', but...'

'I know, sorry. What do you think of... sugar snaps?' Ian was delighted to see her.

'Whatever!'

'Want a coffee?'

'Yes, sure. What were you up to?' Carol settled on the couch that doubled as a bed when uncovered.

Ian prepared coffee in the kitchenette. 'Not much. I am working this afternoon but I don't start till five, so we have plenty of time.'

'Do you want to go out somewhere?' Carol asked absentmindedly as she looked around the place... the way she always did when she came to Ian's as if she had never been there before.

'Sure. I'll get ready after we have coffee and then I'll go straight to work. Where do you want to go?'

'We'll go to my cousin's birthday party.'

'Is your cousin three years old?' he asked.

'No, why are you asking that?'

'It is eleven in the morning. Only kids' birthdays are celebrated at this time,' Ian said.

'No. My cousin's celebrating his thirtieth,' Carol said with a laugh, 'but I want to go early and help them get ready. Then you can go to work. What time do you finish?'

'Ten tonight. But if it is not busy I can sneak out earlier.' Ian looked into Carol's eyes. 'We have some time together before we go.' Ian quickly positioned himself on the couch close to Carol and started stroking her hair. Carol moved his hand with a decisive shake of her head and then pushed him away from her, repugnance colouring her face.

'It's only eleven o'clock in the morning. God, you could do it anytime of the night or day.' Her face suddenly softened.

Ian bit his lip before he could say anything he would regret. *Carol is very picky and can be difficult.* He stared at her, the smell of her perfume was intoxicating.

'Will I get that coffee or not?' Carol finally asked.

'Sure.' Ian covered his disappointment and got up to make a coffee.

'Shall we buy him something?' Carol resumed looking around Ian's place.

'What do you want to buy him? A bottle of good wine? Or maybe a nice aftershave?' Ian said placing a coffee on a stool next to Carol.

'Yes, that's a good idea,' Carol said. 'Oh, either a bottle of nice champagne or an aftershave is a good idea. Whichever shop we come to first.'

Carol drank her coffee as if in a hurry. 'I'm ready,' she said, rising from the couch.

'Wait, I have to put my uniform in a rucksack.'

Carol was still looking around the place, picking things up from the shelf and examining them. She opened a book and skimmed through the pages. 'These letters are funny. What are they like Russian letters?'

'Oh that. Yes. That is Cyrillic. We wri—'

'For Christ's sake, Ian, hurry up!' She put the book back impatiently.

Carol's Morris Minor was parked at the front of Ian's building. 'I wish you had a car so I didn't have to drive you around,' Carol said with a sigh.

Ian bit his lip again so as not to say anything that would cause her to be even more unpleasant; it did not take much to put Carol in a bad mood.

Carol's cousin lived in a typical townhouse in Willesden Green – one in a row of similar houses. Her cousin rented a ground-floor apartment with a couple of friends who were all part of this birthday bash. As they walked into the kitchen, Carol's cousin was busying himself putting ice into a large plastic container already filled with wine and beer. 'Good, you made it,' Carol's cousin said cheerfully. 'How was the traffic?'

'Okay. Are we the first to arrive?'

'Yes, does that bother you?' Carol's cousin paused for a moment and then added: 'Donald's coming in an hour.'

Ian thought Carol blushed at this, and there was short unpleasant moment before Carol snapped. 'Ian, don't just stand there. Where is that bottle of champagne?' She then turned to her cousin: 'Fred, this is Ian. Ian, Fred.'

They then busied themselves with organising tables and chairs and helping to wire the speakers out into the backyard.

'What time does your shift start?' Carol asked.

'Two o'clock,' said Ian, glancing at his watch.

'You won't be late, will you?' Carol seemed concerned.

'It's midday now... maybe you're right. By the time I get to the tube...'

'Yes, you'd better leave now,' she said. 'You'll be back later, won't you?'

'Do you want me to?'

'What sort of question is that? Of course I want you to.' Carol put her arms around him and touched her lips to his. 'See you then, say around ten this evening?'

'Yes.'

Carol always had a distant feel about her and maybe that was something that attracted him. Her Western attitude towards life appeared to be slightly superficial, but it was refreshing for Ian, too. Life was to be enjoyed, not suffered. This attitude was totally different from the tragedies that marred Ian's simple life, but that felt so far away here and with Carol. He needed to work and worry about finances in order to create a better life for himself. He had a future here.

Carol had the common sense of the West; his outbursts of Balkan sentimentalities were often lost on her. She was sweet and light and easy to be with as she didn't complicate life. Conversation usually would solve everything between them.

In that spirit, he took his seat on the tube and opened a book so that he did not have to look at anyone.

Work was busy as usual. He had a couple of hours free between shifts, and went with a few people from work to a nearby café for a drink. They had a laugh, chatting about work and things outside of work. When they returned it was close to seven o'clock – the dinner shift was almost ready. Ian was eager to finish his shift so he could go back to the party. Though tired he knew he could catch up on sleep the next night.

Ian could not read on the tube this time, he kept looking at the map of the stations on the carriage wall to see how much longer it would take before he arrived to Willesden Green.

The party was in a full swing when he arrived. He found Carol in the backyard, sitting and talking to some guy. 'Hi. I made it,' he said bending down to kiss Carol, but she moved her head aside.

'Hi, Ian. This is Donald.' She seemed slightly embarrassed. Was it because of Ian... or because of Donald?

After shaking Donald's hand, Ian sat next to them on an improvised seat. Donald rose and stormed off and Ian was sure Carol looked at him with slight disappointment.

'Why did he leave so quickly? Was it because of me?' Ian asked

'No, don't worry. I am glad you came back.' Carol seemed genuine when she said that. 'It's bit boring here. Do you want to go home?'

'But, I just arrived. Let me have at least one beer.'

Carol nodded agreeably, and her gaze wandered somewhere else.

'Sometimes you are strange,' Ian said playfully.

'I know,' Carol replied off-hand.

Ian thought again that this elusiveness Carol had in abundance was what attracted her to him. She had her own life, she did not need him. Maybe that was why he needed her. He enjoyed his beer, and as he finished he tipped the last drops into his mouth.

'You're shocking,' Carol said with a frown.

'I am, aren't I?' Ian pulled her to him. 'Let's go. My place?'

'We can't go to mine. You know I share.'

'Let's go to my place then,' Ian said happily.

Carol said goodbye to her cousin then turned and gave Ian the car key. 'I'll just say goodbye to somebody else. Please wait for me in the car.'

Ian took the key with hesitation and started walking towards the door. Just before he reached the entrance he turned around and spotted Carol talking to Donald.

As they travelled back to his place, Ian sat back and enjoyed the lights of this big city and the old feel of London. The houses had stood here for maybe centuries and had a feeling of stability about them. This sweet feeling of belonging to this great city pleased him immensely.

When they finally arrived at Ian's Carol went to have a shower – she always kept some of her clothes here. Ian checked his messages: one was from his friend from Bosnia and the other from the hospital where Gina was staying, which asked him to contact them as soon as possible. It was after midnight, but he figured there would be somebody on night duty. So he placed the call.

'Hello, sorry that I am calling this late, but I have had a message from you regarding one of your patients. Gina Maric.'

'Oh, Gina. Yes, I've heard there were some issues earlier on. She is now in the secure unit and sedated. Are you her only relative?'

'I am all she has here,' Ian said. 'What happened?'

'I believe that she attacked another patient today. She has been sedated—'

'Okay,' Ian interrupted. 'When can I come to see her?'

'Well, tomorrow morning would be the earliest. We need someone she is familiar with as she is very mistrustful.'

'Okay, I will be there at around eleven. Is that all right?'

'That's fine. I will let her doctor know, so they can have a conversation with you regarding the best thing to do in the light of all this. She does not have any relatives in London, does she?'

'No.'

'That's not good.'

'Why is that?' Ian snapped.

'Well, it would be easier for her—'

'Well, I am here for her and I will be there tomorrow to see her. Good night and thanks.'

'Good night.'

Ian slammed the phone down, that old feeling of heaviness flooding him again.

'Who were you talking to at this hour?' Carol asked as she came in drying her hair with a towel.

'Gina's hospital.'

'I didn't know she was in hospital. What happened?'

'She had an accident. Anyway, I need to go and see her tomorrow,' Ian said slumping onto the couch and putting his head in his hands.

'Ian, are you crying?' Carol sat next to him, pushing the towel to the side and held him. 'All will be well. You'll see.' Carol held her arm over his shoulder for what seemed an eternity. Ian did not want her to move it. He turned towards her and hugged her.

'Thanks, darling.'

'Now you are making me cry.' Tears welled in Carol's eyes. 'Ian, maybe it's not the right time, but how would you feel if I were to stay here for a few days?'

Ian was slightly taken aback. 'Well, why, but of course.' He paused for a moment. 'Why don't you just move in with me? My place is not very big, but we can find something bigger later on.'

'Thanks, Ian. Yes, I think it's the right time to do this.' Carol's eyes brightened and Ian thought that she felt closer to him than ever before.

They sat next to each other, each in their own thoughts.

'Let's go to bed,' Carol said. 'You need to get up early, and I'll go back to my place in the morning and let the girls know I'm moving out. I could also get some more clothes. I have nothing to wear!'

When Ian woke the next morning Carol was gone. It bothered him slightly that she was not there. He wondered if Carol did not like the place and decided against staying with him, but after showering he made himself cup of coffee and sat down. *Would Carol come back to the bedsit today?* But... maybe she had returned to her flat to collect her clothes as she said she would. His main concern, however, was Gina. He was unsure whether he should contact her parents and explain what had happened. But, that would infuriate Gina, and Ian was sure her parents would have her return home and she would be back at square one.

Ian turned to the sound of a key in the lock and Carol's face appeared at the door.

'Hi stranger!' Carol said, quite chirpy.

'Where were you this morning?' Ian regretted the question immediately as Carol's face changed in a flash.

'Ian, for fuck's sake! What's wrong with you?' Carol was ready for battle.

'I was just concerned when I woke to find you were not there,' Ian said as calmly as he could.

'Yes, and I said I'd go to my place to pick up my stuff!'

'I did not know you would be going so early.'

'I don't have anything to wear, remember?'

'Sorry, sweet pea.'

Carol waved him off. 'Anyway, what time are you going to see Gina?'

'I need to be there at eleven.'

'It's quarter past nine now. You should get moving.'

Ian looked at the watch and sighed. 'You're right.' He finished his coffee and went to get ready.

'Do you mind if a couple of my girlfriends come by here while you are with Gina,' Carol asked.

'Girlfriends? Of course. This is as much your place as it is mine.'

'Thanks, hun.' Carol hugged him lightly and kissed him on the cheek.

CHAPTER VII

London, UK, 1990s

They'd moved Gina to a different room; one she occupied by herself. She was lying in bed and reading some brochure that she quickly dropped onto the small cabinet beside her bed. The brochure fluttered to the floor, and Ian picked it up before he sat next to her bed.

'How are you feeling?' Ian was concerned at the puffiness of Gina's face, no doubt from all the sedatives that they'd given her.

'Terrible. People here are nothing but vile pigs—'

'They are just looking after you, Gina.'

'You must be joking. They treat me like crap. I totally don't matter to them. You know that woman that brought you in here? She is married to an English man who is twenty years older than her. No doubt he brought her from Hong Kong or whatever ping-pong place by mail.'

'Gina!' Ian gasped. 'That is none of your business!'

'How dare you! I have been through hell, and I have the right to express my anger!' Gina was livid, her hands were balled into fist, and spittle caught at the corner of her mouth.

Ian fought the urge to argue, and instead tried a different tack. 'What are you going to do? Where will you live when you get out of here?'

'Can I not come and live with you for a while?' Gina was genuinely surprised, her anger gone as quickly as it had come.

'Well, that is a bit difficult at the moment.'

'Why? Don't you have bedsit with a couple of beds?'

'We'll see when you come out.'

'That makes me feel so bad.' Gina's eyes were full of tears. 'Why have you come here? Just leave.' Gina took her brochure again and turned towards the wall.

'Gina, you cannot just brush aside what happened.'

Gina gazed at Ian turning her head away from the brochure. 'What happened?'

'You attacked a man with knife, you almost ended up in prison—' Ian blurted out.

'Why am I not in prison? I'd rather be there than here.'

'Gina, all I am saying is, this is a place where you should learn to control yourself so that the incident never happens again. You cannot just move on with your life... then all this suffering here is for nothing.'

'You just don't want me to live with you,' Gina spat.

'When are you getting out?' Gina did not answer. 'Gina, Genie girl.'

'Stop with that stupid name calling. Just come next Saturday to visit me. I want to be by myself now.'

Ian was relieved and as he walked down the corridor from Gina's room, the same nurse that brought him to Gina's room appeared.

'Are you leaving already?'

'Well... yes.'

'The doctor would like to see you. You are Gina's only relative here, correct?'

'I am her friend, not a relative. She has no relatives in this country.'

With a nod, the nurse showed Ian to the doctor's office. The doctor did not bother offering his hand, so Ian just stood in front of his desk, waiting to hear why he was called in.

'You are aware that Gina's actions of late point to her not being of sound mind at the moment.' The doctor stared at Ian as if waiting for some sort of response.

'I think that there is nothing wrong with Gina.' Ian was taken aback by his own response, but then after reflection thought that he came out looking like a bit of an idiot doubting the diagnosis of an experienced and educated psychiatrist. 'You think she is not well, mentally?' Ian asked the doctor.

'Her actions in the last period would point to that. Has she a history of abuse? Was she abused as a child?'

'Who? Gina?' Ian shook his head. 'She was not.'

'Okay. It is possible that coming to such a large city as London might have triggered some latent psychotic tendencies. In any case, and keeping in mind the aggression she has demonstrated, I will be supporting the recommen-dation of sectioning Gina under the Mental Health Law.' The doctor perused the file in front of him, and began writing notes.

'What does that mean?' Ian asked.

The doctor looked up from the file. 'It means Gina will be transferred to a mental health ward within the next week where she will be housed for the next three months. She will then be assessed and a decision will be made as to whether she is stable enough to re-enter the community.' The doctor paused and looked at Ian to see if he understood.

With a nod, the doctor continued. 'If Gina improves over the next three months she will need somewhere to stay that will offer familiarity and stability.'

While sitting in the tube, anger rose in Ian. He was pondering different options, but the best one was to call her parents and let them know, let them make a decision. But, he would wait until the three months was up. Gina was sanctioned for three months, not even her parents could have changed that. As the tube came to a stop, he put his rucksack on and proceeded toward the exit. He needed to do dinner shift and was glad it was a short one, where he could leave immediately after.

It was just few minutes past ten in the evening when he entered his building. He held the key of his bedsit in his hand as he started climbing the stairs. Music seemed to be coming from his apartment, and when he opened the door, he was surprised at the number of people in his bedsit.

He searched for Carol, finally spotting her in the kitchenette talking to a familiar-looking guy. Ian put his arm around Carol's waist and she jumped in surprise, blushed for a moment and then turned to the guy.

'This is Ian,' she said. 'You met at the party yesterday.'

'Hi Ian,' said Donald. 'We made ourselves quite comfortable in your home.' With a grin Donald walked away.

'How was Gina?' Carol asked.

'Okay. Well, not really. I don't know,' Ian said absentmindedly.

'Sorry, darling. Are you upset with having all these people around? I think they'll move on very soon. They were planning to go to a nightclub.' Carol seemed to have been looking in Donald' direction.

Ian followed her gaze. 'Have you ever had anything going on with Donald?'

Carol's expression froze. 'No... we're friends. What do you mean?'

Ian then hugged her and added. 'Can't wait for them to leave, so that we can be alone.'

An embarrassed smile seemed to rise to Carol's face, as she let a short sigh.

Gina

A couple of days later Gina was transferred to a new hospital outside London. Ian had not been to visit, and she felt all alone. Abandoned.

The morning after she arrived at the new hospital she walked down the corridor in her dressing gown. At the end of the corridor she found a large room with a television and armchairs. There was a group of people watching television, and she found one empty armchair and sat. She looked around; there was a dark skinned man sitting next to her and he smiled.

'Hi, I'm Cyril. What's your name?' There was something teddy-bearish about him. His face was wide, his cheeks large, and a smile that rounded off his mild and amicable persona.

'I am Gina.'

'And what are you here for Gina?'

'For fun.'

Cyril chuckled with amusement.

'What about you?' Gina did not mind the conversation with this chap.

'Well, I have a history of problems. Just every now and then I break down and feel like punching someone.' He stopped for a moment. 'And I usually do.' Then he laughed again.

'So you are mad? With a certificate?'

'I guess,' he said with a shrug.

They were quiet for a few short minutes.

'How's outside? Can we go for a walk?' Gina asked.

'Once a day with supervision,' Cyril told her. 'All doors are locked. If you wanna go outside with a friend or a relative, they take you out. Even for a walk. Do you have relatives?'

'No. I have a friend.' Gina frowned in thought. 'That is ridiculous not to be allowed outside.'

'We're supposed to be the "heavier" category.' Cyril smirked.

'There is nothing wrong with me,' Gina insisted.

'No, you seem sound as a pound to me.' After a short pause Cyril asked: 'Where's your accent from?'

'What, sorry? Oh, my accent. I am from Yugoslavia.'

'That country doesn't exist no-more. So which part?'

'I am from Bosnia.'

'That's bad. Is your family affected?'

'Affected how? Like affectionate?' Gina said confused.

'I mean has your family suffered as a result of the war?' Cyril said patiently.

'No, they have not. We are Serbs living in a Serbian part of Bosnia.'

'Muslims, they suffered there proper, didn't they?'

'I am suffering here far more.'

Cyril did not ask any more questions after that. He went and made Gina and himself cup of coffee, and they watched a television program that had been chosen by the staff.

Nights were the worst. Gina would wake in the middle of the night feeling heavy pressure in her chest. The walls were closing in on her. *I am a failure. Instead of being a success I have failed. I have nobody around me. I am alone and have nowhere to go. Ian has to help me. I need him.*

Gina would toss in her bed until she was exhausted, and would fall asleep only to wake moments later with the same vision of the tunnel that she was living in... that seemed to close tighter and tighter around her. Sometimes she would cry, and this would relieve some of the pain, make her feel a little lighter.

Thoughts were racing through her mind with urgency and without the need to be solved or even understood. It was impossible to solve her problems. There were just too many. She had to turn to somebody for help, and Ian was the only person who could work it all out. He was her salvation, and it was Ian who could give her the way out she needed.

In the morning, she sat in her bed unwilling to get up. Still feeling tired from poor night's sleep. Somebody knocked on the door, and she called them in.

'Good morning,' said the nurse with the appalling dental work. 'How are you feeling? Still in bed?'

'I didn't sleep well.' Gina could not be bothered having conversation with that creature.

'You need to get up,' the nurse said. 'It's nine o'clock, and you'll miss your breakfast.'

'Could you bring it to me?' Gina asked.

The nurse, obviously used to all kinds of requests, just shrugged 'I'll see what I can do,' she said and walked out.

After a short while, somebody else knocked on the door. 'Can I come in?' she heard Cyril's voice on the other side of the door.

'Yes, come in.'

Cyril walked in with a big grin on his face. 'How're you feeling, gorgeous?'

'I slept terribly last night. Do you take those pills they give us?'

Cyril seemed a bit puzzled. 'Well, yeah, that's the whole idea of us being here. We take pills, "do our time" then leave. Isn't it?'

Gina did not say anything. She just pointed to the chair next to the window.

'Don't you take them?'

'Take what?'

'Pills. You don't take pills?' Cyril asked but obviously did not expect an answer, as he asked another question almost immediately. 'Have you had breakfast?'

'The nurse will bring it to me,' Gina said with certainty.

'I wouldn't bank on it. Now, get up, get ready. I'll meet you outside fresh faced, and we'll go and get you something to eat.'

It was Saturday, and she was expecting Ian to come and visit. It looked like a fine, sunny English day she knew would not be too warm. She took a jumper from her room and sat in a lounge room waiting for Ian. Soon she saw his smiling face as he entered the room.

'Hi. How you are doing?' he asked.

'Crap.'

Ian made a face. 'You have to try harder, Gina.'

'Try harder with what?'

'With trying to make yourself feel better. To get out of this situation.'

'Ian, can we go out for a coffee?'

'Are you allowed?'

'Of course I am allowed with a visitor.'

'God, the situations you put yourself in!'

Gina stood. 'Let's go.'

They spotted a nurse and she seemed to recognise Ian as a visitor, so she pulled her card out and opened the heavy security door. 'On the way out just report to the reception,' she told Ian.

They walked into the warmish English day then down into a small village with a pub on the corner that Ian suggested they try. There was a bar opposite the entrance and a number of draught beers on tap. Ian approached the bar while Gina went to one corner and found seats near the window.

Ian came back with a pint of lager and a glass of juice for Gina. 'So, how are they treating you in there?'

'Ian, I want to get out. Can you tell them that I will stay with you after I leave the hospital?'

Ian fidgeted uncomfortably. 'Gina, I don't live by myself anymore.'

'Who do you live with?'

'Carol moved in.'

Gina slumped back into her seat. 'Well, I am on my own now.'

'Pretty much.'

Gina glared at him. 'What am I going to do now?'

'Gina, you are a thirty-three-year-old woman. You need to make your own decisions. I can come and visit you; I can help you find an apartment—'

'I know how old I am,' Gina snapped. 'It is not my fault that I am in this situation. You know very well how nasty and abusive my father was.'

'My father was an army officer, too. They were all a bit off.'

'Your father was a lovely man in comparison with the nasty things my father did.'

'Gina, you are exaggerating. You were always demanding more than he could give you, and he was professionally accustomed to discipline. You're twisting—'

Gina pushed the glass and some of the juice splashed over the table.

Ian just shrugged and took a sip of lager. After her initial anger Gina went quiet, pensive, so Ian tried to discuss her problems. 'You are constantly angry, Gina. You are not controlled by your father anymore. You are free to do as you wish.'

'But, I don't want to do as I wish.'

'Well, then you need to find somebody.'

'I was hoping you would be that person,' Gina responded angrily. 'Carol doesn't love you anyway.'

'How do you know that Carol doesn't love me? You've hardly spoken with her.'

'I'll tell you some other time. Ian, I need your help.'

'Tell me now,' Ian said then added: 'I will help you. But there are things that I cannot do for you.'

'Just like my father. I will help you, and then he goes on, and I don't see him for days.'

'Is that how he was abusing you?'

'You just don't know how it feels when you love somebody and they are not there when you need them.'

'You don't love me, do you?'

'What are you talking about Ian? Love you? I need your friendship; that is all.'

'You have my friendship.'

'Yes, but I can't get out of here sooner, so I have to wait for the hospital to find me some dingy apartment.'

'You are a grown woman, Gina. You need to learn to look after yourself.'

'I am not capable of looking after myself. Not now. I've been through a major mental crisis, you know!'

'Do you want me to tell your parents about this?'

'No. I will manage.' Gina had an angry mask on her face so Ian thought if she smiled now her face would crack. They finished their drinks without much conversation and when they walked back to the hospital and reported to the reception, Ian hugged Gina's rigid body.

'I'll see you soon.'

Gina walked away as if he did not exist.

'Here comes my friend.' Cyril smiled big grinned smile showing two rows of strong white teeth against the dark complexion of his face. 'Come, sit with me.'

Gina approached Cyril and sat. 'It is lovely outside.'

'Where did you go?'

'Just to the pub with my friend Ian.'

'Has he told you much news about home?'

'No, we talked about other things. Cyril, I want to get out of here and never come back.'

Ian walked to the station dragging his feet. He felt laden with guilt. He was aware there was little he could do, and he certainly did not want to lose Carol. Maybe he could talk to Carol and organise for Gina to stay with them for a short while.

When he arrived home, he put the kettle on and took his mug from the drying tray as he heard a key turn in the front door. Carol appeared and he went to her and kissed her. 'Hello, my love.'

'Hi, Ian. I didn't expect to find you at home? Was everything okay at the hospital?'

'Hmm, yes and no.'

Carol gave him a puzzled look. 'What's wrong?'

'Sit down and I'll tell you.'

He made his coffee and tea for Carol then told her the story in the lightest possible way.

'That's fine Ian,' she said. 'I understand. I'll just go back to my ex-flatmates.'

'But, I don't want you to leave.'

'We can't all fit here Ian.'

Ian slumped back on the couch and as he looked at Carol, the expression on her face was business-like.

'You've got to do what you want to,' she said.

'But we just started living together.'

'Ian, it's only temporary. I'll be back.'

She took his face in her hands and gently kissed him on the mouth. Ian realised that maybe this was not such a bad situation after all. It was only temporary.

Carol stood.

'Where are you going now?' he asked.

'To see my flatmates to organise my going back. The sooner the better. I want to make sure that my old room doesn't get taken.' She slammed the door behind her.

Ian sat a short while longer before calling the hospital to sign Gina's release papers. 'This is only temporary,' he repeated.

Carol

It felt strange to ring this doorbell rather than just get the key out and open the door. In any case, Carol waited and then saw her old flatmate Marty look out the window.

'Hi, Carol. I'll be right down.'

Carol walked into her old flat. 'I didn't know you weren't alone.'

'Oh, we're having a little party,' Marty said and nudged Carol further into the room where a few friends were sitting around.

Carol blushed when she spotted Donald. 'You're here too.'

'Yes, I'm afraid so,' Donald said with a cheeky grin.

Carol made a quick decision and sat next to Donald.

'So, how's life?' Donald turned to her, showing what she thought was real interest.

'Nothing special.'

'It's not what I've heard.'

'What have you heard?' Carol shifted in her seat nervously.

'Well, you know...'

'Well, I know what?'

'You and that Bosnian geezer.'

'Well, if I were with the "Bosnian geezer" I wouldn't be here, would I?'

'Does that mean it's finished?'

'Is that what you'd like to hear?'

Donald eyes widened for a moment then he leaned back in his armchair and seemed to contemplate something.

'Bit of silent treatment now? I like my man to be sure of what he wants.' She stood.

'Wait, don't go.' Donald reached out with his hand, and Carol sat back next to him.

There was a short silence, still Carol did not utter a word. 'Well, how do you feel about us... hooking up.' Donald held her gaze.

'Why not.' Carol gave him a smile that said and gave more than that.

Donald put his hand on hers as a sign of silent agreement. She left his hand there. 'Will you come to my thirtieth? I guess you will, now?' Carol nodded and they both burst out laughing.

'This is hysterical,' Carol spat out between the fits of laughter.

Marty then announced that they should all go to the pub in Covent Garden before going to the concert nearby.

Sarah, sitting at the end of the sofa stood and put her hat on. 'Are you coming with us?' Sarah asked as she turned to Donald and Carol.

'I wasn't planning on it.' Carol looked at Donald.

'I'm not going,' Donald said with the certainty that he already had some plans.

Marty, in the middle of opening the door and letting few friends out turned to Carol, 'Did you want to come?' he asked, noticing that only Carol and Donald were now left in the flat. 'Have you picked up all your stuff?'

'Is my room free?'

'Sure it is. Listen, I'll be off now. Donald, you're not coming either, are you?'

Donald shook his head. 'I've got some things on, but I'll see you at my birthday party.'

'Absolutely,' Marty said before closing the front door.

When they were alone, Donald grabbed Carol's arm, and they kissed.

'Donald, I'm, not ready for anything more than this.'

'I wasn't suggesting anything.'

Carol smiled at Donald's comment. 'Do you want a cup of coffee?' Carol headed for the kitchen.

'No, but I'll join you in the kitchen.'

'Oh, it is so lovely in here, Donald. Plenty of space. A Separate kitchen. Just great.'

'Was the place you shared with Bosnian gee... bloke very small?'

'I hardly lived there. A couple of weeks.' Carol looked at him 'I feel sympathy towards him.' Carol looked away then turned back to Donald and noticed smirk on his face. 'I don't love him,' she said.

'I understand. I mean I didn't mean to interfere...'

'You're not interfering. That really has nothing to do with you.'

Donald nodded. 'Just as long as you're not two-timing me,' he said, then smiled as a thought seemed to cross his mind.

Carol nudged him, 'What are you thinking of now?'

'Nothing, just if you two-time me, then we'll have to have menage-a-trois.'

Donald ducked away as Carol swung her arm at him lightly. 'Enough of that nonsense,' he said. 'Let me make you a cup of coffee to make up.' Donald opened the cupboard and grabbed a cup.

They sat on the sofa with cups in their hands. Carol leaned against Donald's shoulder. 'This feels good,' she said quietly.

'What did you say?'

'Nothing. Coffee is good. But in the future make me tea, I prefer tea.'

'I better get going,' Donald said as he stood.

'Okay then, if you must.' Carol left her coffee cup on the table and stood too.

'You have things to do, I guess. Do you need any help with moving?' Donald said.

'No, I'm fine. Majority of my stuff is still here. But, thanks anyway.'

'Okay then. Well, I'll see you on Saturday at my party.' Donald turned to her and put his arm around her waist. He softly pulled her closer to him and kissed her gently. He took strand of her hair and kissed it. 'I like your hair.'

Carol smiled at him. 'See you Saturday.'

Only when Donald left did Carol realise the situation she was in. Her gut was telling her that being with Donald was more natural, and Ian would survive. She wouldn't tell Ian about Donald, just distance herself from Ian and let him find out eventually.

Carol turned the key in the door of Ian's bedsit and walked in. She jumped in fright. 'I didn't expect you here.'

'I live here.' Ian was sitting on the sofa that turned into the bed.

Carol felt suddenly scared that Ian knew about her and Donald. She approached Ian and sat on the sofa next to him. She took his hand and looked him in the eyes. 'I do love you and always will.'

'Why are you saying that? Are you leaving me?' Ian looked gobsmacked, but then his expression changed to normal. 'Are you?'

'I came to get the rest of my stuff.' Ian's expression changed again into surprise. 'I mean some of my stuff.' It crossed Carol's mind that Ian didn't suspect anything. She wasn't sure if she was relieved. Maybe this was the right moment to say something. She stood, and another thought entered her head: *I like Ian and I don't want him out of my life.* She now felt totally divided.

What's the right thing to do? I guess I'll just need time to work this one out for myself.

'Of course I'm not leaving,' she told Ian. 'Why are you saying that?' Carol rested her head on Ian's chest and stretched her arms around him.

Ian didn't hug her back.

Carol let go and went to the wardrobe and started packing.

'It feels as though you are leaving for good,' Ian said.

When Carol turned, she couldn't see any signs of understanding of what was going on.

'What's happening with Gina?'

'The usual,' Ian said.

'Will she come to stay here?'

'Why are you asking me that? Of course she will.'

'I don't like when you're snappy.'

Ian sat with a grim expression on his face, silent.

Carol put the bag down. 'What's going on Ian?' She'd never seen him this down before.

'Nothing. Just go.'

Carol felt uncomfortable just leaving. She sat silently next to Ian instead.

'I am not looking forward to Gina coming here,' Ian finally said.

'Then let her stay somewhere else. Let the hospital find her somewhere.'

'It is easy for you to say that. It does not work like that in our culture.'

Carol didn't say anything. *Your culture and my culture… that is our problem.* 'Then let her stay with you until she gets better.'

Ian remained silent for a while before finally admitting. 'Gina will not get better. That is the way she is.'

'Sometimes life just works things out for the best if you leave it.' Carol tried to be positive and to help Ian get out of the rut he was getting himself into.

'I guess that is the only option I have. Don't worry about me. We will still see each other.'

There was no answer from Carol.

'We will see each other?'

He turned to Carol who decided to stand at that moment, and as she had her back at him she responded, 'Of course we will. Why wouldn't we?'

As she continued packing, her eyes filled with tears. All that covering up of emotion had to come out. She was glad she still had some work to do so there was enough time for her eyes to dry. As she finished, she looked around and was pleased she could survey it with a couple of glances.

'I think I'm done, Ian.' She looked at him as he started pottering around the place.

She stood watching him, deciding how to do this. Then she went to him, hugged him tight, she raised her head and found his lips, they were familiar and soft, she kissed him and it felt good. She let go and turned to grab her bag. On the way out she heard him utter, 'Bye, see you soon.'

Carol closed the door behind her. There was an empty feeling and uncertainty in her. She wished she could tell which one of those two emotions was stronger.

CHAPTER VIII

Momir woke feeling a hundred years old. Every bone in his body ached. He looked around still unaware of where he was. There was an incredible stench in the air, and he searched for its source. It was the filthy mattress he was lying on in a cellar-like room.

There was a small square opening covered in iron bars at the top of the wall close to the ceiling of this hole of a place. He stood, feeling as if his bones were crushing around his lower back. He stumbled as another bolt of pain shot through his upper back around his shoulders. Propping himself up, he looked through the iron bars and saw pavement. *Below ground.*

He looked back at the room, trying to work out where he was. The mattress took up one third of the room and there was an equally dirty UNHCR blanket on it.

He dropped his head to his hands and held it for what seemed an eternity. How did this happen? Momir shook off his disbelief and begun searching for his rucksack. There. On the floor against the wall. Opened, some of his possessions were hanging out if it. The sight of the rucksack revived his memory.

His dream of escaping besieged Sarajevo ended a few hundred meters from the apartment where he'd lived for the past two long years.

Three soldiers brought him into this abandoned police station, which now bore strange writing and an unusual coat of arms. His disappearance into his mother's flat had sheltered him from the outside world and its current machinations… and he'd suffer because of it.

He vaguely remembered being shoved and kicked with heavy boots; one blow to his lower back had been the contributing factor to the crushing pain he was feeling.

The men were making fun of him, indiscriminately kicking him to keep the animosity high. Strange place in these strange times.

The big, burly soldier hit him the most; Momir had dubbed him the 'executioner' of the group. The wiry soldier was too nervous and unsure of what was the right thing to do. The third one, quiet, uninterested or possibly simply resigned to Momir's fate.

During the 'interrogation' Momir could not help but think that maybe this was better than hiding in the apartment and waiting for God knew what. Something was happening; he was out among the people, in the real world. Regardless of how bad that world was. The Executioner took vociferous notes as Momir answered all their questions. It was then Momir realised they were not from Sarajevo.

Momir did not feel scared. All of this reminded him of the bullies in high school. Still it was best to get on their good side to elicit as light punishment as possible.

He finally managed a good look at the logo on the arm of their uniforms and realised it was some sort of Bosnia and Hercegovina army official signature; although he wondered if they were the official Bosnia and Hercegovina Army, and to which country's army the other two belonged. Serbian and Croatian soldiers? No point in starting the debate now.

They'd said that it would take few days for them to find him something 'useful' to do, something to further the efforts of the Bosnian army. Momir was not sure if he was sorry he'd been caught. At least he was talking to people other than his mother. His mother. How could he let her know how he was? She would be worried if he didn't manage to contact her.

He needed a cigarette, but couldn't find his stash in his rucksack. He knocked on the door; knocked harder when no one came. Pounded on the door until he realised nobody was coming. He grabbed the iron bars and shook them – nothing.

'Anybody there?' he yelled. 'Hello. Can I talk to somebody?'

Nothing.

Momir slammed his hands against the door in frustration. He wasn't a prisoner in his Sarajevo flat anymore but a proper prisoner. He slumped onto his mattress and then sprawled across its length.

A key turned in the lock.

The heavy door opened.

'Were you thumping on the door?' A scrawny-looking man in a green uniform asked.

'I was,' said Momir as he stood. 'Do you have a cigarette?'

'What do you think this is? The Hilton?' The man looked at him with disgust. 'Where did they get you from?' the man asked before turning around and locking the door, not interested in an answer.

'I tried to leave Sarajevo. I think it was yesterday when I was brought here,' Momir called after him.

'And why didn't you bugger off from Sarajevo?' The man turned towards Momir and gave him another look of disgust.

'They were better than me I guess,' Momir said.

'Of course they were better. We are a proper army. We are taking Sarajevo and the Americans are with us. Remember that.'

'I understand that now. How long will you keep me in here?'

'As long as we need to.'

'Do you actually know?'

'I sure do.' The man's smile was cruel.

'Could you tell me?'

The man studied Momir, anger growing in his eyes. 'You will go out to the front and dig canals for us in a few days. You won't be sitting here for free, I can tell you that much.' The man turned away on the words, and Momir listened to the dwindling footsteps.

Momir lay on the mattress and studied the room before finally going to the small window. With deliberation he shook each bar. One seemed to move. There was a piece of cement missing from where the top of the bar was fixed into the wall. Momir scratched around it with his nails, but that wouldn't work. He checked his rucksack but anything he could have used to pry the bar away or use as a weapon, had been taken. Even the buckle of the rucksack had been cut free. They'd left the sandwich his mother had prepared for him, and although squashed and bruised it was still tasty.

Tonight he'd try and loosen the bar.

Momir was woken up by rattling at the door. When he opened his eyes, a man stood at the door holding a tray with a metal bowl on it. The man's uniform was shabby; his jacket had a couple of buttons undone, and the laces on his boots were undone.

Momir raised himself into a sitting position. The man did not say a word, but Momir thought he looked familiar. 'Here's your meal,' the man finally said. 'Do you want to have it here or ...' The man looked around the room, realising there was nowhere else to have the meal handed the tray to Momir.

'I know you from somewhere,' Momir said without looking at the man.

'We all know each other from somewhere,' the man said as he headed to the door.

'Wait. Talk to me. Please.' Momir put the tray on the floor and all of a sudden remembered. 'Didn't you live in Dobrinja?'

The man looked at him totally unfazed. 'I still live there. Although it is a bit worse for wear now.'

'I live... lived there. Street Rade Koncar.'

'There are no Rade Koncars anymore. It is all Green Beret this and that, and liberators this and that, although I am not sure whom we are liberating ourselves from.'

'Do you know how much longer will I be here?' Momir asked; the man was definitely not interested in discussing memories.

'I don't know, my son. I only do food and clean a bit. Talking about cleaning; how's your pot?' He went to the corner, removed the pot and closed the door behind him before returning a few minutes later and with an empty pot 'You will be taken to the front very soon. You will be digging canals there. That's what all of you do.'

'Thanks,' Momir said as the man left.

The soup bowl was full of some reddish watery substance with beans and onion floating in it. There was a quarter of bread next to it. The soup was not as bad as it looked. *Did the man make it?*

Momir was surprised at his complete lack of emotion, or regret for finding himself in this situation but it was better than hiding in the flat with his mother as his guardian. He was ready to start digging the trenches. Anything was better than the uncertainty of not knowing.

Momir was confused when he woke, but the lingering stench in the room reminded him soon enough. When was the last time he had a shower? Last Thursday; the night he left the apartment and his worried mother.

Momir hoped his mother wouldn't start worrying seriously about where he was for at least couple of weeks. It had to be Monday today; there had been more commotion outside yesterday with the mosque rituals that Muslims had suddenly started observing.

Keys jingled in the door.

A man entered. 'Pack up. You are leaving here this morning.'

'Where to?'

'Just pack up and make it fast.' The man stood at the door waiting for Momir to get ready.

Momir grabbed his jumper from the end of the mattress and zipped up his rucksack. 'I am ready.'

The man walked over to the kibble. 'Are you leaving this for me? I don't think so. Grab this and on the way out we'll go to the washroom and you'll empty and wash it in there.'

Momir did as he was told. He put his rucksack on the shoulder and with the free hand grabbed the kibble. 'Lead the way, old man.'

'Go through and then to the left.'

Momir walked into a small corridor with walls of exposed bricks; the stench was coming from the nearby toilet. They walked through some dark corridors until they reached the end of one that widened into a washroom.

'Where do I empty this?'

'Certainly not here. Leave your rucksack here, we'll come back.'

Then the man took him outside where there was a building with a toilet hole inside. 'Go in there and throw it into the hole and then get water in this bucket,' said the man, showing Momir a metal bucket, 'and empty the bucket into the hole.'

Momir did as he was told; dumping and washing the kibble as instructed. All the while the man watched on. After this ceremonial was finished, Momir was allowed to wash. He stripped and splashed himself generously with cold water and was grateful for the small piece of well-used laundry soap; it would not lather, but still made a big difference in his attempt to cleanse his skin and remove some of his stench.

'Okay, stop your beauty routine, and let's go.'

Momir followed the man out to the front of the building where he was handed off to a guard.

'Here he is, the Serb they caught the other night,' the man said despite Momir trying to get his attention.

'Thanks,' Momir muttered.

'C'mon, no time for goodbyes,' the guard said, ushering Momir forward with a rifle. 'There, through that door.' He pushed Momir again.

A man dressed in uniform was sitting at a desk covered in paper, books, and files. He had his hand on a piece of brown paper with some white cheese and piece of bread in it.

'Commander, this is the latest prisoner, one for the trenches.' The guard pointed to where Momir had to stand before taking a position next to the door.

The commander looked up and then grabbed a small piece of bread and some cheese and stuffed it into his mouth. He nodded as he chewed and opened one of the folders then took a pen.

'Chetnik, ha.' Without waiting for an answer he added while still finishing last morsel of his nourishment 'What is your full name?'

He diligently wrote all of Momir's personal details into the book. 'Have you been enlisted to the Serbian army?'

Momir was hesitant: 'I was, but after a short stint I was discharged for medical reasons. As a matter of fact, it was JNA army.'

The commander looked up with a piercing stare: 'How long was that short stint?'

'Six months.'

The commander wrote something into 'Momir's' page. 'Caco, take him outside and lock him up. This evening a small group is going up to Igman, and I'll let them know to come by and pick him up. He will come in handy.' He looked up at the guard as if to make sure the instruction was understood. 'Dismissed,' the commander said, then buried his head into his paperwork.

The guard took Momir by the elbow and pushed him through the door, and then to a small cell. 'What's the matter? Scared?' the guard sneered.

'I don't know what to expect.'

'Well you won't know until you get there,' the guard said as he closed the cell door.

This was a proper cell with yet another dirty mattress and a blanket. Maybe he was better off with his mother in their apartment. Would he see his mother again?

Consumed by his thoughts, he fell asleep.

He was startled awake and found a different soldier at the door to his cell.

'Have I woken you up?' this guard asked sarcastically.

Momir said nothing.

'Grab your gear and come with me.'

He followed the man to a desk where Momir's name was ticked off before being led outside where he joined a group of men in possibly same situation as him who were being guarded by another soldier.

They were herded forward into the dark. None of the prisoners spoke, and once darkness descended he could no longer see their faces. They were leaving Sarajevo city behind and moving towards the outskirts, towards Mojmilo.

'Be very quiet now,' one of the soldiers whispered as they got closer to the prisoners.

Momir almost enjoyed the walk and he tried to remember the last time he was here. A picnic with friends. He'd got slightly drunk. It was good. They'd had a lamb on a spit roast and when he closed his eyes he could still taste it.

'Oy, you, stay in the line,' one of the soldiers whispered at him.

It was pitch-dark. They were walking uphill between oak trees. Momir did not feel tired and he gave no thought as to where they were going. While he knew the area quite well, it all felt new and foreign.

Suddenly words were exchanged ahead. Not from the group of prisoners.

'We are bringing some prisoners with us.'

'How many?'

'Three.'

'Okay.'

The words that followed were directed at Momir and his two brothers in arms.

'Move in front. Faster.'

Momir was pushed with the rifle barrel. They walked between two trees that looked like an opened door where sacks were piled to make walls. They were moved behind one of the sack walls and directed to something resembling a wooden shed.

'Stay there.'

Momir sat on the grass, and the other two prisoners dropped down, too. They seemed as puzzled as Momir but they also carried exhaustion and helplessness in their expression.

'God knows what will become of us,' said the eldest-looking prisoner.

'Where did they get you?' Momir asked the man.

'I was—' The butt of an automatic weapon was stuck against the man's back.

'Keep quiet! You're not on a picnic here.'

A look of understanding passed between Momir and the other two prisoners, and soon a guard came back from the shed and they were led towards the forest where they came across more sacks and a short shallow trench.

Two soldiers seated on the ground looked up at Momir and his 'brothers'. Covered in dirt and dust, only a few spots of white were visible on their faces. 'Where do you want them?'

Momir and his fellow prisoners were directed to shovels and a shallow trench. The guard then lay beside the trench, automatic rifle in front of him, and did not move.

Momir and the other two prisoners started digging, slowly, each lost in their own thoughts. The position was above the forest and perfect for defence. It would be impossible to be attacked from below as any move would be absolutely noticeable. The small shed was slightly removed from the forest. Momir realised this was to be the frontier of a Muslim-held area.

They were still digging when a new day broke. Rays of light bathed the trenches and prisoners and soldiers, the forest was oblivious to what was happening around them.

Momir wondered how much longer they would be digging. He could smell his sweat but knew that soon he would not be even able to do that. A few bullets ruptured the air and Momir automatically lowered himself even further. The Muslim soldiers did not react. Momir's heart rate intensified, but he continued to dig all the while trying to make himself smaller somehow.

They were still digging hard while the sun crested the sky – it had to be noon. He thought of his mother for a moment but quickly diverted his thoughts. When his shovel hit a rock, he would dig around a rock to release it, and then he carried on doing what he was told: digging a trench big enough to lie in.

He thought of the absurdity to dig for Muslims but again this thought was only fleeting as his only concern was to save himself. A couple of hours later a man came with carrier bags and some pots and bread in it and they were allowed to break to get something to eat.

The other prisoners already looked spent, their shirts were sweaty and their shoes covered in dirt. Their faces were dusty and it was caked in their hair. Like the other men

Momir gulped his food down. One of the soldiers offered them a cigarette and Momir took it with appreciation.

They were only given an hour of rest late in the afternoon but they all fell asleep quickly. When Momir woke it was dusk and the other two prisoners were staring at him with a look of horror in their eyes.

'What did you dream of?' Momir tried to make a joke.

A different guard called for them to get up and carry on digging. 'You have few more hours of work and then around ten you'll go back and sleep behind the shed.'

All three worked with a renewed energy and by the time the guard told them they could stop and come with him, they were exhausted. They were shown small covered area with a couple of metal beds and some blankets on it. All three took a bed, a soldier remaining with them, smoking as he gazed toward the forest.

Momir awoke amid loud voices. He did not move, just opened his eyes and took few seconds to realise where he was. The guard was gone and the other two prisoners were still sleeping.

Momir tried to decipher the voices, and from what he could tell, there seemed to have been an action.

Run.

This is a perfect time.

He reached under the bed; his rucksack was still there. He quickly removed a jumper and pulled it on; shoved his feet into shoes then stood, rucksack in hand.

'Where are you going?'

Momir dropped his rucksack. 'Nowhere.' In the dark, he could still see a silhouette of the guard.

'C'mon. Get the other two up and come with me.'

Momir woke the other two, and feeling deflated shoved the rucksack under the bed and went to the guard, waiting for the men to join him. He grabbed his shovel automatically.

'You won't be needing that,' the guard said, directing them to the front of the shed were some soldiers rested in a dishevelled state.

There was definitely an action last night.

'You three, grab this stretcher and come with me.' The guard shoved them towards a stretcher where a soldier lay with an obvious gunshot wound that was bleeding freely. The soldier was quietly weeping.

Momir grabbed the front of the stretcher and tried to stay in step but the wounded soldier's boots kept hitting him on the thighs.

The soldier's breathing was coming in short gasps, but they continued to struggle with this heavy load before finally reaching what looked like another barracks. *Must be the ambulance station.*

'Straight to the front door,' the guard said, holding it open.

There were ten or so beds sprawled around the room and a few women were tending to the injured men. A couple of doctors, recognisable by their white overcoats, were moving between patients.

One of the doctors approached and examined the patient on the stretcher. Momir and his fellow prisoner were still holding the stretcher.

'This man is dead,' the doctor said, the dark circles around his eyes seeming to deepen at the pronouncement.

Then he turned to Momir. 'Bring the stretcher to that bed,' he said, pointing to one of the rare vacant beds.

The doctor motioned to another man tending to one of the patients: 'Help me to move him from the stretcher.'

Momir looked at the dead man. His expression was vacant, his face ashen. Momir quietly whispered: 'Amen'

Spring turned into summer. Under different circumstances Momir would have enjoyed it, but as it were, this summer was the saddest of all. Unable to contact his mother, he knew she would be worried sick. He had tried to approach different guards a couple of times for help but to no avail. They could not care less about a Serb prisoner and his needs. They had enough needs of their own.

His days were spent digging trenches, cleaning up after actions, carrying the prisoners and occasionally peeling potatoes. Constant uncertainty became as natural to him as breathing. But the consistent gunfire was difficult to bear, as was the feeling of being surrounded by strangers who spoke his language.

Then one day he overheard Muslim soldiers talk about something very enthusiastically.

He approached one of the men as they were having their dinner.

'What's happening? What's the happy news?'

'Americans will bomb your Serbs,' sneered a soldier.

There was a sense of celebration in the air amongst their Muslim captors from then on; a sense that they had won the war. They were celebrating with greetings of

Selam as if that single word gave them a sense of security and national identity.

Momir did not feel defeated.

They were happy, and from then on seemed to treat the prisoners a little better. Morale within the Muslim troupe remained high well into early autumn, then Momir learned they would be exchanged for Muslim prisoners. Momir's uncertain and dreary existence would be replaced with a shuttered existence – the apartment with his mother.

On the day of prisoner exchange, he woke early. Milan and Bosko, his fellow prisoners were already up.

'Who are you hoping to see at the prisoner exchange?' Momir asked.

'I don't know,' said Milan, 'I don't know where any of my family is or if the Muslims have managed to contact them.'

They gathered what few belongings they had and sat on makeshift beds waiting for the call to start moving. To an observer they would have looked much older than they were. Being only in his thirties, Momir already had quite a grey mane on his head; he would have let his beard grow but his captors were always reminding him to shave it off – they told him he resembled a Chetnik too much and they would have had to kill him. This would inevitably be followed by Muslim soldiers' loud and raspy laughter.

At around noon a guard ushered them out and they retraced their journey. It felt lighter this time – a sense of returning to where he belonged; back to the security of home.

He'd provided his mother's details as a person of contact, but had not been told if she would be there. Still he was on the move. He would not be sleeping on a makeshift bed in stables behind the village house; he would not be washing from a bucket. Momir was very pleased he did not have to spend the winter here. That would have been torturous.

They walked through the carpet of fallen yellow leaves. In better days, he would have been kicking through while enjoying the shuffle of leaves, but now the walk was an ordeal. As they came out of the woods a large meadow spread out before them. In the distance two large groups of people stood opposite one another. *The prisoner exchange site.*

As they neared, soldiers stood before a group of prisoners. Momir and his friends were told where to stand, two mates here approached one of the soldiers in the group and obviously had Momir and his mates registered. Then he turned and pointed, and after checking their papers, the guard left them there then chatted with some soldiers before disappearing.

'He didn't even say goodbye,' said one of Momir's prison-mates.

Momir and the other prisoner smirked at each other then returned to searching those at the other side of border trying to recognise one of their own.

A Muslim officer started a roll-call of Serb prisoners; a Serb soldier following with the name of a Muslim prisoner. They would then cross sides and head into the group of civilians where cries and kisses and hugs would start.

Momir's name was read out towards the end, and he crossed to the other side oblivious to who was freed in exchange. He approached the group of Serb civilian soldiers hoping to see his mother when a weak hand grabbed him by the elbow and bony arms encircled him. He moved back to see her face. 'Mum? It is you!'

He grabbed her and held her with as strong a grip as he could muster to show her that he was not a broken man.

'You are all bones!' His mum was shaking with excitement and kept kissing him and stroking his arms and shoulders.

'Are you still in the flat?' Momir asked.

'I am.'

'Let's go then,' he said with a smile. 'Has the shooting died down?'

'Since the NATO bombing there are hardly any shootings. Serbs had to move to the Pale side only. They completely lost control of the city. Forget about that. How are you? You have lost so much weight.'

They clung to each other like two broken birds and went on towards their apartment.

Melbourne, Australia, 2000s

Tanya woke the next morning feeling quite confident in her search for a full time job. Even before having a cup of coffee she went out to get the newspaper. Once home, she put the kettle on and began searching the employment section of the paper. There was one interesting job: a tourist agency that was part of a large chain. She dialled the number.

'Hello, I am calling regarding the advertisement in the newspaper.' Tanya tried to sound no-nonsense while keeping to her best English.

'Oh, yes. The person you're after isn't in the office right now. Would you be able to call later?'

'What time would be the best to call again?' Tanya asked.

'Around lunchtime if that suits you.'

'Of course. I will call back. Thank you.'

Tanya made herself cup of coffee and after taking a first sip her phone rang.

'Hi, it's me,' Goran said. 'How are you doing?'

'Not bad. Do you want to meet today?'

'Sorry, babe, I have something going on today. Maybe tomorrow?'

Tanya was annoyed; Goran always seemed too busy to meet. *What is he busy with? He does not have a job.*

'Have you found something work-wise?'

'No, I'm trying, though. I am meeting with a friend who might be able to give me some work. Afterwards, I should take him for a drink.'

'Why should you take somebody for a drink if they are helping you with a job?'

'Please don't annoy me. I have enough on my plate as it is. I am stressed to my eyeballs!'

What are you stressed with? Obviously it is not work since you do not have a job. 'Just calm down,' Tanya said regretting her negative thoughts. 'Everything will be fine. You will get something. I believe in you,' she said trying to settle the nerves on both sides.

'Okay. I'll talk to you later. Will you be at home?'

'Yes.'

'Talk to you then.'

A sense of futility overwhelmed her; a feeling so strong it left her gasping for breath. She had to keep calm and try not to annoy him and create a difficult situation between them. But inside her, there was a volcano ready to erupt.

Is this really who he is? A confused little boy who does not know what he is doing? I don't believe that he can change to become more mature. He was simply not in the mood to go out, but underneath she felt that something was not right about the whole thing. His attitude left her feeling edgy and made her appear needy.

She walked aimlessly around her apartment before sitting back down and resuming her search through other job ads in the newspaper.

Every few minutes her thoughts would wander, she would have sip of a coffee and then resume. When she glanced at the clock it was quarter past noon. She dialled the agency number with renewed vigour. *I will give it my best.*

'Hello, my name is Tanya and I am calling about the job ad. I have already tried earlier but the person looking after the position was not available–'

'Oh yes,' said a friendly female voice. 'So you would be interested. Have you worked at a travel agency previously?'

'Yes, I've worked at an agency for about six months, it was a contract work. I also have degree in Serbian and International literature. I have travelled–' Tanya started explaining carefully.

'Let me see… could you come Monday at two pm?' the female voice asked.

'Absolutely,' Tanya answered.

'You know where we are?'

'Yes, I have the address from the ad. Thank you so much, and see you on Monday at two pm. Who should I ask for?'

'Nela. I will interview you with another colleague. See you Monday.'

That night she tossed and turned for a long time before exhaustion finally overtook her, and when she woke, she felt much better about Goran. As if on cue, her phone rang.

'Hiya. Did you sleep well?'

'Goran! Yes I slept well. How was last night?'

'I sometimes feel as if you are interrogating me.'

The tension was back in an instant. 'Will your job come through?' she finally asked.

There was a pause on the other side 'Taaanya. You are interrogating me.'

'Sorry. Do you want to meet?'

'Listen, babe. I'm not sure how things are going to work out today, but I'll give you a call in the afternoon, and let you know. Is that okay?'

'Sure. I might be out so maybe leave a message,' Tanya said as nonchalantly as she could.

'I'll call you in the morning then.'

'No, call me today. I really would like to see you today,' Tanya said trying not to sound too demanding or needy.

'Why don't we just organise now to meet at six in front of the Palace cinema in the city, hey?'

'Yes that is a good idea.'

'Finally! Miss you already and see you at six,'

Tanya was just about to say something when the line went dead.

When they met that evening, Tanya had forgotten all the little squabbles of the morning and relaxed into the ease of being with him. Their troubles seemed so far away in these moments.

'Do you ever use as an advantage the fact that you come from Bosnia?' Goran asked as they were sitting in a bar, pleasantly decorated in dark wood and vintage glass.

'Not really. I do not like saying that I am from Bosnia. I often say that I am from ex-Yugoslavia. That was where I was born.'

'I would use it if I were you.' He opened his wallet and showed her the flag of Serbia, protected in a plastic pocket. 'I would have fought for Serbia. I had fights with people over Milosevic. But now I've lost all zeal to defend it anymore.'

Tanya was stunned. 'You cannot do much all by yourself. On the other hand fighting with people over beliefs is futile.'

'You don't understand,' Goran said.

'I do understand.'

'Let's drop the subject.' Goran sounded irritated again.

Tanya felt uncomfortable; she wanted to please Goran, and what she had said about fighting for beliefs, she thought sounded condescending. 'I was condescending. I did not express myself well...'

Goran wasn't listening, he was glancing around the bar. 'Look at that girl! She walks like she owns the place.'

The girl was very pretty, and when Tanya looked back to Goran his gaze was on anything but her.

Tanya felt empty inside. Sometimes she wondered if she could actually disappear into her subconscious, to find a place where a piano played all her favourite overtures, where she immersed herself in the comfort of fine food and good books.

'Shall we go?' Goran was already standing.

'Sure. We just need to pay.'

'Have we not paid? I'll get it,' he said. 'Did you drive here?'

'Yes. I parked a bit further away,' she said. 'Would you walk me to the car?'

'Sure. I'll walk you to the car and then catch a bus home. I have to get up early.'

Tanya did not complain about this; in a way, she was pleased to be alone that night. She would read a book and maybe get some of that smooth feeling of contentment to return.

In the morning, Goran called quite early. 'I didn't sleep well last night,' he told her.

'Is something worrying you?' Tanya said, knowing she had to show concern, as that seemed to work with Goran.

'I spoke with my mother, and my dad is ill.'

'That's terrible! How old is your dad?'

'Around sixty.'

'What is wrong with him?'

'He has some sort of flu and high temperature.'

'But that is normal. I mean it is common to have the flu. It is winter up there now.'

'You and your pragmatic viewpoint!' Goran said angrily. 'He hasn't gotten out of bed for a week now.'

'That is bad,' Tanya said, reverting to concern again. 'Do you want to meet today?'

Goran sighed. 'Maybe in the afternoon. I'll come to your place around four.'

'Okay. See you then.'

Tanya already felt a bit flat. Still, she busied around the house and tried to make a cake so that they could have it with a coffee.

Goran arrived just after four pm and she could tell immediately he was in a good mood.

'What's going on?' Goran slouched on the couch and grabbed a book from a coffee table. Without waiting for Tanya's answer, he said 'I didn't know you liked Proust?'

'I like a bit of heavy reading now and then.'

'Proust isn't heavy. He's complex.'

Tanya bit her tongue; Goran was very protective of literature and considered it to be his territory. She did not want to fight with him.

'I'm going back to Serbia for a while,' Goran told her.

'When? Why?' Tanya sat, her body feeling like it weighed a tonne.

'I'm going in three-weeks' time. I bought a ticket this morning.'

'But you did not ask me.'

Goran looked at her with amusement 'Why should I ask you?' and then seeing Tanya's face moved closer to her 'I didn't mean that.' He pulled back. 'I have to go. My mother thinks I'm better off there.'

'But Goran you are a grown man, your mother cannot decide what is best for you. And what about me? What about us?'

'What about us? I'll come back. It is not forever.'

'When are you going to come back?' Tanya asked, still trying to process the news.

'I don't know exactly. Please don't annoy me. I have too much on my plate.' Goran reclined on the couch and opened Proust and engrossed himself in its pages.

The conversation was over. Still, she felt as if somebody had thrown a bucket of cold water over her. She felt cold and emotionless. It felt like the relationship with Goran had ended the minute he'd told her he was going back to Serbia. He could have walked away; she would not ever go looking for him. He left soon after, still in good spirits.

Goran called every morning as was his normal habit. 'Are you upset because I'm leaving?' He must have finally got some understanding as to why Tanya had become cool. 'I will be back.'

Tanya did not even bother to ask when.

She finally told him over the phone a couple of days before he left for Serbia that it was over between them.

'How can you do this to me?' Goran seemed genuinely in shock.

'Do what to you? You are leaving, not me.'

'I will be back. Oh, don't worry. Just go back to your sad life and become an old maid.'

Tanya hung up; there was nothing she wanted to add.

She returned to her solitude. Some days she was angry at how naïve she had been, but other days she thought that any friendship gives one something. But it takes away, too. This time, she thought, she had given more than she had received. This did not bother her – she was not very good at taking. Maybe one had to value oneself highly not to give more than one took.

Summer was nice in Australia with beaches and places to enjoy the good weather. Tanya went to cafes and places where women of her age danced, reminding her of dying swans – there was desperation in their moves, as if they did not dance for their own pleasure but for onlookers and prospective partners. This made Tanya feel uncomfortable. Maybe she was too old for this scene now.

She went to Serbian church one day and met with an only mutual friend she and Goran had.

Tanya gave Vesna a genuine smile. 'How are you Vesna?' Tanya asked kissing the woman's cheek.

'Goran's still in Serbia?' said Vesna.

Tanya did not know what to say to that so she said nothing.

'I am going there for holidays. When are you going overseas?'

'I don't know,' said Tanya. 'Soon. Goran and I had broken up before he left.'

A look of hope, Tanya thought, crossed Vesna's face. 'He asked me about you?'

Tanya was bit annoyed with this. 'I don't know why.'

'Don't you think that you were cruel to him?'

'No.' Tanya turned and left, never had she been so sure that she should not pursue a relationship with Goran.

A few weeks later another friend said to Tanya, 'A friend of mine waited for her boyfriend, who later became her husband, for two years while he was overseas.'

'How old was your friend when her future husband left her waiting?' asked Tanya in sudden lingering judgement.

'In her twenties I guess,' the woman thoughtfully recalled.

'Well, I was forty-one when Goran told me that he was suddenly going to Serbia,' Tanya said.

'Age doesn't matter. If you love somebody you wait for them,' the woman assured her.

'I guess you do,' Tanya said with resignation and took a sip of her coffee, observing young people pass by on the sidewalk outside the café.

CHAPTER IX

London, UK, 1990s

Gina was very pleased to be leaving this godforsaken hole. There was a sense of apprehension about what was to come, but she had Ian to worry about these things that would trip her up again... the same things and worries that had brought her to this terrible place.

Gina checked the time: ten minutes past noon. Ian was supposed to pick her up at noon. She went straight to reception and asked if they could call Ian to ask why he was not here.

'You need to wait a bit longer,' the receptionist told her. 'Maybe he's caught in traffic.'

'He is always on time,' Gina insisted. 'Can I just leave then?'

'No, you cannot leave without your caretaker signing the document of release.'

'Damn!'

At that moment, Ian walked in, red in the face. 'Sorry. Bus was late and then the traffic was terrible,' Ian apologised.

'Whatever,' Gina said, not hiding her annoyance.

Ian's face darkened with Gina's comment. Nevertheless he went to the reception desk and asked to sign papers and complete any other formalities. The receptionist gave him three pill vials, each with instructions attached. Ian thanked the receptionist, grabbed the vials and ushered Gina out.

They were quiet as they sat on the bus heading to London, and it was Gina who finally broke the silence. 'Finally I am out of that terrible place. Now I can finally have a normal life again.'

'I hope you've learned something through all of this and that you'll change your behaviour,' Ian said.

'What do you mean?' Gina said defensively. 'It is not my fault that I ended up in that stupid place?'

'Whose fault was it then? Was I to blame?'

'You could have helped more,' Gina stated.

Ian looked at Gina's face for signs of her joking, but Gina was lost in her own thoughts. Her face was calm and showed deep signs of suffering. It angered Ian although he stopped himself from having an argument with her. He knew there was no point; Gina was not going to change her mind. But he was not going to change his either.

As soon as he could he would help her find a place of her own so he could get on with his own life. His thoughts turned to Carol; he'd give her a call as soon they returned home. He missed her. He missed her free spirit and lack of obligations to anyone but herself. There was something very freeing about the Western way of life.

'Ian I would like to learn to drive. Can you help me with that?' Gina asked out of blue.

Ian frowned. 'Do you know how much each driving lesson costs in London? Where will you find money for the car? You don't work.'

'I'll find a job,' Gina said.

'I don't think that you're in position to look for a job now,' Ian said calmly.

'Why not?'

'Yes, you are right. Find a job.' Ian sat back admiring the surroundings through the window and his thoughts returned Carol.

As Gina unpacked, Ian went downstairs to the communal phone and called Carol.

'Hi, it's me.' Ian was delighted to hear Carol answer the phone.

'Oh, you're back.' Carol sounded surprised.

'We just returned.'

'What is Gina doing?' Carol asked.

'Unpacking.'

'So what's the plan?'

'I don't know yet.' Ian did not want to discuss the details with Carol at this stage.

'Okay. Was the trip difficult?'

'No, it was okay. How's your ne... old flat? Are you settled in?'

'Well, it doesn't feel as if I was away at all.'

'Well, don't get too settled,' Ian said with a small laugh.

The silence on the other end of the phone made Ian uncomfortable. 'Carol, this isn't going to last too long.' Ian turned to make sure the door of his bedsit was closed. 'She will move out soon.

'Okay, Ian, I understand. Just do what's best.'

Ian hung up feeling a gap forming between him and Carol. He didn't want that gap to deepen.

Gina was in the bathroom when Ian returned. When she walked out, she was dressed to go out.

'Are you going somewhere?' Ian asked.

'I am going out to look for a job,' Gina said seriously.

'That's bit too soon. You need to get well again first.'

'I am well,' Gina snapped.

'Gina, you are not well. You are on the dole at the moment, so you have means to survive. Once you get a job you would have to get off the dole, and it will be difficult to return to the dole as it would take time and effort.'

'I need a job. I have to be independent.'

Ian felt resigned to whatever Gina wanted to do; she was a grown woman. Still he made one last attempt. 'Have they assigned you a social worker?'

'Yes, she is coming here next Wednesday.'

'You gave her my address?'

'Of course. This is where I live now.' Gina sounded more reasonable than Ian did.

Gina grabbed her bag, checked the contents and then asked Ian. 'Will you be here when I come back? I don't have keys.'

'Take these ones. Carol's left them.'

'Carol was living here?'

'I told you that before, don't you remember?'

She ignored the question. 'Okay, I am off. See you later.' Gina was already out the door.

Ian checked the time; it was four o'clock already, and he had to get ready for his dinner shift. He'd told his Manager that he would be late for work that day, so he had time.

By the time he returned home that evening it was already close to eleven. He unlocked the door quietly and saw that Gina was asleep in his bed. He'd agreed to sleep on the sofa, so Ian was happy that at least one thing was right. He dropped his rucksack, removed his jumper, changed shoes for slippers and took the towel before heading to the bathroom.

After having a shower Ian went back to his bedsit and stretched the bed sheet over the sofa, grabbed a pillow then lay down and covered himself with the blanket wishing Carol was here.

Ian was woken by Gina opening cupboards and clanking mugs in the kitchenette. He opened his eyes and saw Gina putting a kettle on. 'Make me cup of coffee too, would you?' Ian said with a yawn. 'What's the time?'

'Almost seven-thirty,' Gina answered happily.

Ian blinked the last of sleep from his eyes. 'Why are you up so early?'

'I am going to work,' Gina said with a proud smile.

'Wow, that didn't take you long. Where is the job?'

'Cleaning job,' Gina said.

'That's good.'

'There's your coffee.'

Gina pottered about the place for another five minutes then left. Ian lay in bed, thinking of Carol. He must have dozed off because when he looked at the clock again it was nine am.

He wondered if he should call Carol but didn't want to come across as desperate. Either way he dressed quickly and went downstairs to the phone in the foyer. He grabbed the phone and started dialling the number but he put the phone down before he finished. *Why doesn't she call me? Well, I asked her to move out. But, I had to. She should understand that. Maybe I should give her a call. I want to see her.* He grabbed the phone and dialled the numbers with confidence this time.

A male voice answered the phone.

'Hello, it's Ian. Could I please talk to Carol if she is in?'

'I'll check if she is in her room. What did you say was the name?' the man asked.

Ian waited for what seemed to be an eternity. He was getting annoyed; this was his girlfriend and he was made out to be some stranger.

'Hi,' Carol answered in a happy tone.

'Hi, it's Ian.'

'Oh, it's you. My friend said your name wrong.'

'Who is he?'

'Oh, just a mate of mine. He doesn't live here.'

Ian wanted to ask why the hell her "mate" answered the phone if he didn't live there, but he stopped himself. He just said: 'Carol, I miss you. I would like to see you.'

'Well, come over. Or, hmm no. I'll come to your place. Is Gina there now?'

'No, she has gone out to work.'

'She works?' Carol couldn't hide her surprise.

'Well, she wanted to get a job. Maybe that would be good for her.'

'Okay. Well, I'll see you in an hour then.'

Carol sat herself on the sofa while Ian made coffee. She looked around for traces of Gina; she wasn't sure how she felt about this swap of places. 'How did you find Gina's behaviour now that she is out of hospital?'

'It's too early to say, but I have a feeling that she has not changed much,' Ian said as he poured milk into a mug.

'Well, that's not very good. I guess you expect her to be quite different. Cured, perhaps,' Carol mused.

'Well, she is not a piece of ham to be cured.' Ian was bit annoyed with her comment, but Carol did not seem to take offence.

'I know. I didn't mean it that way.'

'Did you miss me?' Ian tried to be amorous as he sat next to Carol.

'I was quite busy the last few days,' Carol said and reached for her cup of coffee.

'Too busy to think of me?'

Carol moved away slightly and faced Ian. 'Ian, do you think that... we're going to work?'

Ian was taken aback. 'Why wouldn't we?' he cocked his head. 'Have you met somebody?'

Ian took small relief from seeing how Carol's face lightened. 'Not really,' Carol answered without pause, 'but it's hard to be on a standby with you.'

'You are not on a standby.'

'You don't know how long this thing with Gina is going to take? It might be weeks or months or years,' Carol said.

'I am under pressure. I cannot let go of her now. She needs me.'

'I find your tribal connections a bit hard to take.'

Ian was quiet for a moment. 'My background is important to me.' Ian turned to face Carol. 'It's what keeps me grounded. You need to accept that my background is different to yours. I understand your background. I guess it is easier for me as I live in this society now, and I am happy to take it in, but I have to keep some parts of myself from my old world, it's my core.'

Carol fidgeted uncomfortably as she listened to Ian present himself in this way. She leaned over and kissed him. Ian was surprised but responded, forgetting about his vulnerabilities as if the raw nature of his being bounced back to take this offering.

Carol

Carol heard a knock on the door, and after calling on somebody to open it, realised she was in the flat by herself.

'Donald, what a surprise!' She opened the door to let him inside. He kissed her on the mouth as he walked into the flat.'What are you up to?' Donald was dressed in jeans that looked as if he just bought them and dressy shirt hanging over the top of them.

'You're all dressed up. Are you going somewhere?'

Donald looked puzzled. 'Are you having a laugh?' Donald shook his head with a smile. 'What's up with you? Does the name Prince mean anything to you?'

Carol stood there for a moment then her eyes went wide. 'Oh, the concert. Of course. What's the time now?' Carol searched for a watch.

'Ten to six. We have to be at Wembley at seven-thirty. The others will be waiting at the main gates for us.'

'I'll get ready quickly,' Carol said and hurried away.

'You better,' Donald called after her.

As Carol was getting dressed she thought of Ian briefly. *I'll make up my mind when the time comes.*

Ian

Ian was happy to spend the night inside his bedsit. Memories of Carol's visit today were enough to keep him content; everything was good between them. He did not want to lose her.

He looked at the watch and realised it was already eight pm. He had not seen Gina since that morning and surely her cleaning job could not take that long. That disturbed him. He should not have let her go.

A key in the lock and a dishevelled looking Gina walked into the bedsit.

Ian could not help himself. 'Where the hell have you been?'

Gina looked bit embarrassed for a moment but then regained her fighting spirit. 'Who are you, my mother?'

'Gina, you are not well. You just came out of hospital.'

'You know very well that there is nothing wrong with me. I was in hospital because of stupid laws.'

Ian took a calming breath. 'Okay, okay. So, where have you been all day?'

'I was looking for an apartment. I want to move out.'

'You should wait until you get better—'

'I am well.'

Ian studied at Gina; her hair was a mess, there were dark circles under her eyes and her clothes were torn. She had a large fake leather bag on her shoulder that obviously had all that she needed for the day in it. At the back of his mind, Ian could not help but think that he would not mind being on his own again. This would mean that he could ask Carol to move back in with him.

'So, were you successful with finding a flat?'

'Yes. I'll go back tomorrow, get the keys and organise the payment through the dole.'

'Okay, it's your decision. And you're a grown woman.'

Gina grimaced then went to her suitcase and begun to pack. 'Will you ask Carol to move back in?'

Ian was surprised by the question. 'Maybe. Is that a problem?'

'No, it is your life.' And after a short pause while still knelt over her suitcase with her back to Ian, she added: 'although, she does not love you.'

'Why... Why are you saying that?'

'Forget it. Don't worry.'

Ian thought it best not to answer. Gina hardly knew Carol; her opinion would be driven by her selfish motives of having Ian to run back to if she had nowhere else to stay.

Ian worked the early shift the next morning and when he returned Gina and everything she owned was gone.

He sat on the sofa feeling flat but the first thing that crossed his mind was to call Carol. He went downstairs and dialled her number, but it went straight to the answering machine.

'Hi, this is a message for Carol. It is Ian. Could you please give me a call when you get a chance? Okay... talk to you soon.'

Ian was slightly unnerved. It would have been nice to have talked to Carol – she was his bright star at the end of the dark tunnel. With that thought, he put his feet up and dozed off.

Carol

As they danced and sipped beer from plastic glasses, Donald was becoming very affectionate. He lifted Carol at one point, and they kissed. When he put her down, she looked around and realised that everybody was enjoying themselves too much to notice the two of them.

'What's wrong, honey?'

'Nothing. I think I'll go to the bathroom.'

'Now?'

Carol was already on her way as she waved to him. 'I'll be back soon.' She moved slowly towards the bathroom and after a long queue at the toilet she was finally inside. She took a moment to look at herself in the mirror. *Make a decision! Make a decision! But, I'm not getting married to Donald. Still, I mustn't let the moment... oh who cares. After all, it's Ian's fault for letting me be by myself.*

She finally got back to Donald and put her arm around him while hitting him with her hip. He responded in kind.

Carol woke in the morning, grabbed her wristwatch as she struggled to make out the numbers on the small dial. All she could see was that the smaller hand was on ten. A smile crossed her face when she thought of Donald. Coffee with him around noon today would be just perfect. Nothing was promised. No boundaries were crossed. It was neat. She stretched lazily then got slowly out of bed. She showered, dressed and donned her favourite leather jacket before heading out.

She walked into a cafe at around eleven-thirty. She was lucky to find a table next to the café window. She ordered breakfast and thought to have a coffee later when Donald arrived.

That half an hour went by quickly, and soon Donald's smiling face appeared at the door. He kissed her before taking a seat opposite her.

'Did you have something to eat?'

'Yes, but you go ahead and order. I'm ready for coffee.'

'No, we'll have coffee.' Donald motioned to the waiter and then turned back to Carol 'So, what are you up to? It was awesome last night.' He then stretched his torso as he leaned leisurely at the back of the chair. Carol smiled; he was so charming and easy to be with.

Late that evening Carol returned home; she felt quite good about the early afternoon she spent with Donald. She then looked at the answering machine and clicked on the messages. Ian's voice brought her back to reality.

She sat down heavily and let her head hang backwards. The only sensible thing was to call Ian. There was heaviness in her fingers as she dialled his number, quietly hoping he would not answer and, therefore, give her more time to enjoy present situation.

But he answered, breathing fast. 'Hello?'

'Hi Ian, it's me. How are you?'

'I've got some good news,' he said.

'What is it?'

'Gina has moved out.'

'So soon! But where?'

'She's found herself accommodation.'

'But, will she be all right?' Carol was in shock, this changed everything. Carol was not even listening to Ian's explanation. She knew that she had to act and think quickly. What now?

'..so, would you?'

'Sorry, what did you just say?'

'Would you be willing to move back in with me?'

'Oh Ian—'

'I know that I have stuffed you around, but—'

'I know it wasn't your fault. Listen Ian, let's leave this for a week, and I'll sort myself out and give you a call.'

'But why, I mean—'

'I have to organise rent so that I can get my bond back and all other financial things. I don't want to just lose all that money.'

'Sure, I understand.'

Carol put the phone down feeling at odds. She felt a strong attraction towards Donald and thinking of him made her feel alive, but Ian was stable and there was a strong sense of reliability about him. She did not want to lose that. She lay down on her bed staring at the ceiling. Her phone rang again and she knew it was Donald. She let it ring out.

CHAPTER X

Banja Luka Region, Bosnia, 1990s

Momir woke to an early autumn morning and a musty, unpleasant smell. He opened his eyes then closed them again. He did not want to be here. He looked around the room; his mother's bed was empty.

The makeshift kitchen was empty too. His mother was out again. A feeling of helplessness enveloped him; he did not feel like leaving his bed. But then he thought of his mother and raised himself into a sitting position. He looked for his slippers and not wanting to touch the floor with bare feet stretched his leg to pull them closer. He put the slippers on and got up.

Kids' laughter from the outside broke through his gloominess. He checked the time, nine-thirty in the morning. He was a thirty-five-year-old man who lived in a one room apartment with his mother. But a touch of optimism breezed through him and he decided today he would definitely go and apply for a job with the international community. Maybe his chances were not good as he did not know anybody in this town; after all he'd been in the new place only couple of months.

His mother left the apartment the day he was exchanged. Since then they were given this space in the collective centre, which Momir wanted to leave. Every day he was wandering streets of this now Serbian-occupied town when he met a Norwegian guy in the park. Momir knew enough English to have some sort of conversation with Harald, who gave him his business card and suggested that Momir come see him in the office.

Momir searched his wallet and pulled out the business card Harald had given him. It felt like a gold coin in his palm.

He went to the communal bathroom and cleaned himself rigorously before returning to his room and choosing a shirt and trousers from the UHCR donated wardrobe. A small pat of cologne and he was ready to face the nice autumn day.

He walked down a few wrong streets, but thankfully some passers-by directed him to the NCR. A girl at the reception desk was local, so he did not have to start struggling with English yet. She was not willing to let him see Harald as Momir did not have an appointment, but Momir persisted and eventually the receptionist gave in and called the Norwegian.

After placing the call, she pointed Momir to an office at the end of the corridor. Momir thanked her then proceeded down the corridor, taking a deep breath before knocking on the door and entering.

Harald looked up from his desk and gave Momir big-smile filled with large white teeth. Harald extended his hand as he rose from behind the desk.

'Hey, my Sarajevo friend. How are you doing?'

Momir felt like a grizzly bear in a china shop. The thought of his own yellow-stained teeth stuffed with fillings made him feel very uncomfortable about opening his mouth. 'I am fine.'

'What good have you come to share with me then,' said Harald, still holding his smile and pointing to a chair on the opposite side of the desk.

'Well, I need a job,' said Momir as he took a seat careful not to knock anything off the desk, which was covered with office equipment: pen holders, post it notes, new computer, printer, folder, notepads... there was barely an inch of clear space.

'You need a job.' The smile slipped from Harald's face and he assumed pensive look. 'Well, can you speak English. I guess you can.'

And then as if he was talking to himself, Harald said, 'I wouldn't mind somebody like yourself working here.' And then looking at Momir an even bigger smile rose to his face. 'People like you should be working. You're local; you have the knowledge and experience, yet you are young.'

Momir looked down at his shoes that had definitely seen better days, but before he could say anything Harald stood.

'I know,' said Harald. 'We need a driver. You do drive don't you?'

'Sure I do,' said Momir.

'So what do you think, can you drive me around?'

'Sure I can,' Momir said, hardly believing his luck.

'As you know we're just starting here and I had a driver assigned to me temporarily. He wants to leave, so I'll tell him that I have somebody else. Guess where he's returning to? Sarajevo. You might even know him?'

Momir was quite confused; he was not sure that he understood the whole conversation, but he did get a feeling that Harald was talking about somebody from Sarajevo. 'So you have a job for me? In Sarajevo?'

'No. You will be my driver. But we might drive to Sarajevo every now and then, who knows?' Harald laughed lightly and then nodded to Momir. 'Today is Thursday, how about you come on Monday bright and sharp at eight am?'

Momir just looked at him not sure if he understood well enough. He had a job.

'Right, your salary will be about twelve-hundred German marks. Is that okay?'

Momir heard the amount of money that Harald mentioned, and he understood that this was the salary for the job, but he wasn't sure what period of time would he have to work for that money.

He didn't want to come across as cheap and talk about money at this stage. And then it dawned on him. *Is all that money for just one month! That amount of money, for a month?*

'Thanks a lot. You want me to start next week?' Momir said in a deadpan voice in order to cover his excitement.

'Yes, next Monday at eight-am, sharp. Eight o'clock in the morning, okay?'

Momir stood and held his hand out. 'Thanks a lot, sir. You will be happy with me, I promise.'

'I know,' said Harald with a smile as he opened the door for Momir. 'Oh, and brush up on your English by Monday.'

For the first time since the beginning of the war Momir felt light and optimistic. He hurried home to give the good news to his mother. *She will be delighted.* He found his mother in the communal bathroom washing his trousers in the basin; her hands were swollen and looked like two pieces of over-risen bread. She glanced up when he called to her and smiled her crooked, gap-toothed smile.

'Mother, I've got a job at the International Organization!'

'Really?' She dropped the wet trousers into the basin, dried her hands on the ends of her light dress then she hugged him tightly. 'Well done, my son. Well done!'

He went to bed that night feeling that he accomplished something. He had made somebody else happy, too.

Monday morning Momir fairly leapt from his UNHCR donated bed and did his morning wash-up routine, elated. He arrived at work fifteen minutes before his start-time and when he walked into the office, Harald was already sitting at his desk just like the day Momir had first walked through the door.

'You're here, nice and early.' Harald did not get up from his desk but pointed Momir toward the kitchen. 'Make yourself cup of coffee and then come back here so I can take you through your day.'

'I am okay,' Momir told him. 'I don't need a coffee. I had one already.'

'Okay, suit yourself. Come here then.'

Momir found a chair and sat waiting patiently for Harald to start explaining Momir's job.

Harald moved his chair to face Momir. 'Right. Today I have a meeting with the mayor. You will need to drive me there. After that, we'll come back, and then you are free until the evening. Your job will be to look after the car, making sure there is enough petrol in its tank and that the car looks clean,' he said. 'If the car breaks down or if it needs service you need to take it to the base where our mechanics will look after it.'

Harald looked at him and Momir nodded his understanding.

'On Friday we will need to go to some villages in...' Harald then looked through his papers. 'Japra-Valley?' he then looked at Momir. 'I have been there; we have maps so it will be easy to find. We have four-by-four Landrover, which will easily go through any terrain. So far, all is good?'

'Yes, no problem.' Momir felt like a part of a team already.

Harald then looked at his watch. 'Right, go and check that there is enough petrol and that the car looks good. Here are the keys.' Harald handed the keys to Momir, 'and I'll meet you there...' Harald looked at the watch again '...in an hour when we will be going to the Municipality Office to meet with the mayor. Oh, one more thing, I have an interpreter, she should be here at eight. Her name is Boba, and she is local.'

Momir nodded. 'Okay. I will leave you alone now,' he said, happy to get on with his job.

As he opened a door, a young twenty-something woman stepped past him and into the office. She had a long dark hair with a fringe, dark trousers and a white shirt, and good-quality leather shoes with small heels.

'Morning,' she said chirpily.

'Morning Boba,' Harald said.

Momir shook hands with Boba. 'Hello, I am Momir, the new driver,' he said by way of introduction.

'Hi, I am Boba. Welcome,' she said.

'Thank you. I believe we are going to the municipality today. I'll just go to the front and check the car.'

'Okay,' she said with a smile, 'Come back to the kitchen when you're done and we can have a coffee if you like.'

'Okay. Deal,' said Momir.

Momir's first day was full of strong impressions. He drove them to the meeting and waited in the car in front. The local policeman allowed him to stay there once he understood the car was part of an international organisation.

It took Momir a short while to get used to the routine of driving to different places and waiting around for Harald and Boba to finish their meetings.

The money was good, and soon he and his mother were very financially comfortable. They finally decided to move out of the collective centre and rent an apartment. Momir gave his mother most of his salary as his job took him away for almost all of the week, and sometimes on the weekends he would go to Zagreb with Harald and Boba and others from the organisation.

On one such trip they went to Split, on the coast, and Momir got to talking with Boba more than he usually did. Harald and his Norwegian friend were drinking somewhere together, so he and Boba had plenty of time to themselves. He knew she was in a relationship with one of the Internationals, but he was not on the trip with them at the time.

'It feels as if it is "us and them" doesn't it?' Momir said.

'How do you mean? You and I and the Norwegians?'

'No,' said Momir. 'Back in Banja Luka, locals working for the Internationals are different from the rest of the local population.' Momir took a sip of his juice and briefly looked at the waiter serving drinks at another table. There was a slight breeze from the sea bringing salt to his nostrils. There were people strolling down the walk next to the sea. Tall street lamps were alight.

'I don't really care about that. They would all work for the Internationals if they could,' Boba said bringing him back to conversation.

'Sure they would. The money is excellent; and the work is okay.'

'Yes, but the work is not going to last forever,' Boba told him.

'Are you very serious with your International?'

Boba could not stop laughing. 'Yes we are very serious. We live together.'

'That does not mean serious,' Momir said with a smile.

'You are right. But his mission ends in six months, and then he will go back to England. I will go with him.'

Momir figured this would be the case. Boba was not a stupid girl, she knew her worth. 'Do you have a problem understanding each other? I mean, after all, you are from two very different cultures.'

'No, not really. I find him very civilized and he is capable of looking after me. I don't believe there are many locals that can give me that sort of security in life.'

Momir took his time and then puzzled said, 'But do you love him?'

'Do I love him? Of course I do. I wouldn't be with him otherwise,' Boba said.

Momir didn't want to pursue questions about the depth of Boba's love. 'I think I saw him with you on one occasion. You do give the impression of a happy couple.'

Boba didn't comment.

After a short pause in which both glanced at the people on the terrace, Momir said. 'Are your parents in Banja Luka also?'

'No, when Knin fell, I left with my aunt and my parents were in a different car. I stayed in Banja Luka with my aunt, and my parents proceeded to Serbia. They eventually ended up on the outskirts of Belgrade in a collective centre. After about a year of living like that, they managed to buy small house in Vojvodina. My father is a very good tradesman, so he builds and does all the plumbing for the houses. They are okay.'

'Do they know about your boyfriend?'

'Yes, John and I went to Vojvodina so that they could meet each other.'

The waiter came by their table and they looked at each other and ordered another drink. When the waiter left Momir said. 'So this is really serious then.'

'Yes, that's what I told you.'

Momir smiled. 'It is nice here.'

Boba nodded. 'I love the Croatian coast. The smell of the sea and the relaxed atmosphere. Aaah.'

They both laughed as the waiter bought fresh drinks and removed empty juice bottles.

'After everything we went through I never dreamed I would be sitting here on the Croatian coast having a relaxed drink,' Momir said.

'True. After all, they threw us out of Krajina,' Boba said without bitterness.

Momir's face took a serious expression. 'Was the falling of Krajina terrible?'

'Awful. We left in one day. Out of the blue. Our neighbour told us the night before the Croats were cleaning out Krajina in a big operation and all the Serbs would be thrown out of their houses and shoved out of Croatia.' There was a wet sparkle in Boba's eye.

'Like garbage in spring,' Momir said with a shake of his head.

'Except it was August.' Boba assumed her normal composed look for a moment. 'I was only twenty-two when that happened, but still the fear was palpable. You don't know what to take when you only have a few hours to pick the things most important to you.' Boba looked away from Momir.

'So what did you take?' Momir said quietly.

'Photographs. I thought that was the most important.'

'I guess you are right,' said Momir, thinking back to what he'd put into his rucksack when he'd tried to flee. 'Why didn't Serbs stay and fight?' Momir posed a question which he knew was too large to ask Boba.

'Who would fight? Ordinary people. We did not have arms,' she said. 'Where was the Serbian army?'

'That is a good question,' Momir said with a bitter laugh. 'I guess the whole episode of Krajina had the smell of a sale.' Momir shook his head. 'Us Serbs, we always sell something, but we never have anything,' he glanced at Boba and resumed the thought after he detected puzzled expression on Boba's face. 'Except the top politicians, maybe they are making profit from all those sales.'

'I guess that is why they have the money.' Boba smiled sarcastically. 'They must be the ones doing the selling.'

'We are so divided, us Serbs. That is why we lost the war.'

Momir walked into their rented apartment late that evening. His mother was still awake. 'What are you doing up this late? I hope you were not worried for me?'

'No, all is fine,' his mother said with a small smile. 'Sit down, I have something to tell you and I could not wait till the morning.' She took a breath. 'The neighbour told me about an apartment in the centre of town. A man who owns it went to Serbia, he is from there originally, and because he is an army man he got another apartment in Belgrade. He wants to sell this one, and the price is very good. Only 28,000 German marks. I have saved fifteen thousand—'

'How did you save fifteen thousand?' Momir asked, surprised.

'From the money you were giving me,' his mother said matter-of-factly.

Momir was astonished. 'And you never said anything?'

'Momir, don't worry about that now. I have asked my sister, and she and her husband will lend us the rest. We will pay them back in two years' time.'

Momir begun to laugh. 'That's great, Mother! And that price... that is really cheap for an apartment in the city centre!'

'I will go there tomorrow as the owner is in a hurry to sell. He already lives in Belgrade wants to arrange everything tomorrow.'

'I'll come with you,' Momir said.

'No, you go to work. My sister and brother-in-law will come with me. So you are happy with this?' she asked.

'That is excellent, Mother.'

EPILOGUE

London, UK, 2000s

'**M**aark! Maaaark!' Celine's yelling shrieked through the quiet morning in the apartment.

'What?' Mark came in drying his hair vigorously with a towel. 'You're having a baby!'

'You're Einstein! Excellent,' Celine said. 'Quick, get me my maternity bag from the bedroom and let's go.'

Mark threw the towel on a chair and rushed to the bedroom, quickly pulled his trousers and a jumper on and picked up Celine's bag on the way out of the room. 'Can you get up? Do you need to change?'

'Of course I need to change,' Celine snapped, then noticed the angered expression on Mark's face. 'Get the car started, I'll be at the front in a minute.'

'I wish you had your mother here,' Mark snapped.

'I wish I lived in Mayfair, but I don't,' Celine snapped back.

'I think you've done well,' Mark said, his face darkening as he turned to face Celine. 'Don't start now. I didn't mean it.' He put the bag down and approached her.

'How can you say such horrible things?' Celine felt tears running down her face. 'No, don't touch me now, just go and get the car.' She dried her face with her hands.

Mark picked maternity bag and headed towards the door. Celine went to the bathroom and started her beauty routine. After ten minutes she emerged from the bathroom and went to the bedroom looking for clothes to wear. She observed herself in the full-length mirror. A smile brightened her face.

As she settled into the car, Mark took off with the screech of tires. 'Don't drive like that!'

Mark's brows knitted together. 'Not a word. Not a fucking word.'

Celine looked out the window. *London is lovely at night.* 'Are your parents on the way to London?'

'Why?' he stared at Celine's horrified face, then he nodded. 'Of course they are.'

'Where will they stay?' Celine held onto her belly, starting to exhale quickly.

'With us,' said Mark as he focussed on the traffic ahead.

Celine's breathing became more rapid. She opened her mouth to say something, but Mark added. 'I am going away tomorrow.'

'Where?' Celine frowned.

'Celine, I told you this before,' Mark snapped. 'To New York. We're opening a business there.'

'Are you going by yourself?' Celine exhaled few deep breaths.

'Why is that important?' Mark glanced at Celine.

'Just asking.' Celine looked out of the window again.

'My mother will stay with you for a week, and then—'

'And then?' Celine glanced at Mark. 'When will you be back?'

'In two weeks. I couldn't have avoided that, but I've shortened the trip as much as possible.'

'Is that new girl... Charlotte, going to America with you?' Celine observed his face and for a moment thought there was a smile after she mentioned the girl's name. She looked out the window. She could see the hospital. As Mark brought car to an urgent stop and grabbed the handle, Celine put her hand on his. 'Mark.'

'What?' Mark had confused expression on his face.

'Promise me one thing.' She stared into his eyes.

'Go on.' Mark's face lightened.

Celine gazed deep into his eyes. Celine felt her eyes moistened and humility overwhelming her. 'Promise me that one day we will buy an apartment in Knightsbridge.' After a short pause she added, 'a small one.'

Mark looked at her, side of his mouth drown downward; his eyes wide open. 'Are you being serious?' he said as he stared at her.

Celine stared back. 'Mark, I want our child to have the best start in life.'

Mark's face was pensive for a moment. He stared into her face as if examining it. Celine felt as if his whole being was concentrated in the thought that he had at that moment. He finally added as he put his hand on the door. 'Somehow, and in the end, you always make sense.'

Sarajevo, Bosnia, 1990s

Kemal, Selma and Haris, walked into their apartment with their hearts half-filled. The fact that they were only one family of many that had been affected by the war did not help them.

'Son, I made you burek. I know you love it,' Selma told her son.

'Thanks, Mum.' Haris glanced at his grandfather's sombre face and then added, 'I'll eat later, Mum. I am not really hungry now.'

Selma did not insist. She went into the lounge room and lay down on the couch and closed her eyes. Kemal sat on another couch, Haris sitting beside him.

'How are you holding up, Haris?' Kemal managed a smile and then shoved Haris playfully. 'Selma, I will go to the mosque tomorrow and to Merhamet. I will put the word out, and we will find Seid. Whatever happened, it is inshallah,' he said, and then after a short pause added. 'You cannot change Allah's will.'

Selma was silent, but finally opened her eyes and looked at Haris: a tear tumbled down her cheek. She pushed herself up and held Haris against her, breathing in his scent.

'Mum, is there any hot water?' Haris asked. 'I'd like to have a shower. I stink like an old sock.'

That brought laughter to all them. 'Sure there is,' Selma said as she stood. 'I'll get you towels.'

When he was left alone, Kemal's head dropped and tears streamed down his face like rivers. He looked up towards the ceiling and said silently: 'Why Allah? Why?' He then wiped his face with his hands and his eyes were left just slightly red. He then stood and went to the phone.

'Who are you calling now?' Selma asked as she came down the corridor.

Kemal did not answer.

'Hello. Yes, it is me Kemal. Yes, Selam Aleikum to you. My son was not at the exchange... I know... Yes, yes he was... Haris is with us... True. I know many have lost... I know. Inshallah. We will win... If you hear anything... I know you will, but still... Any news at all, any morsel of news, just call me any time of day or night... Yes, I'll come down to the mosque. When? Soon.'

Kemal put the phone in the receiver then turned to his daughter-in-law. 'Selma, I will take Haris to the mosque with me tomorrow.'

In the morning, Kemal was walking down the street with his head held high and a resolution to live with this hardship. To continue on with dignity, as that was what his son deserved. Haris was walking next to him dressed in his Sunday best: crisp white shirt and black trousers that fitted him well. There was a slight tinge of uncertainty on his face as a result of hardship he endured in living in war conditions, and the adventure that even the young do not find adventurous. At least not Haris.

When they arrived at the mosque, there were a lot of people out front. Some were washing their hands and faces at the concrete communal basins, others were talking in small groups or standing and waiting for the prayer to start. Haris sized the mosque with his gaze; it looked solemn like everything in those days. It was quiet, and this was one of few mosques in town that was secluded.

Grandfather went to the mosque often before the war, but Haris thought that his mother was more pious to what she had been since he left.

Grandfather and Haris approached a group of people sitting and speaking quietly on the bench.

'Selam Aleikum, Kemal. How is it going? Is that Haris? Inshallah, with you?' an older, grandfather's age, man accosted them. He was puffing on his cigarette and holding it between his thumb and index finger revealing yellow stained tips of those fingers. The man did not wait for Kemal to answer, but continued looking at what seemed to be his flock.

Kemal quietly whispered to Haris. 'Look at him, behaves like an imam. He has sent both his daughters overseas to Turkey, and married them off well and now preaches to everybody.'

Haris smiled knowing full well that his grandfather would never get over his love of discussing little life nuances, but it was always without any malice.

'Selam, Kemal.' They both turned to the voice. A man, his father's age smiled with obvious look of hardship on his face.

'Mustafa.' Kemal was genuinely pleased to see this man. Kemal hugged him.

'I came back last night. I am going back tomorrow,' Mustafa said while screening the area, then he added. 'Haris you look well, my son.' He hugged Haris. 'Kemal, you and Haris must come for a coffee at my place today. My wife's made shortbread, and it is sweet like it never was. Haris has to meet my daughter. I don't think they ever met. She never goes out. I am worried about her. Just cooks with her mother. Goes to school...'

'That is good. That is how you want your daughters to be,' Kemal said with a sign of approval.

'Sure, but not to that extent. She is an only child that is my worry. She needs to have few girlfriends.'

'What do you know of girl's behaviour; tja.' Kemal waved his hand in dismissal. 'Anyway we will visit you one day.'

'You will come today. No, I do not want excuses I want you to come today. Who knows if I'll come back home after I go this time.' There was a stony silence that followed.

'Don't say that.' Kemal breathed some life into this ominous moment. 'How about if we come to see you today after the mosque?'

'Perfect. I'll wait for you here after the prayer. My wife and daughter will love to see you; I can guarantee that.'

Prayer was quick. Nothing took too long in these days. Kemal spoke to a few more people before they found their shoes. As they were putting them on Mustafa approached them.

'Let's go,' said Kemal as he stood.

They all proceeded slowly and quietly with Mustafa, there were no birds in sight. Most likely they were in some more peaceful place.

The three of them walked one after the other, keeping close to the walls before finally arriving at Mustafa's building.

Kemal promptly opened the front door of the building and went inside. Haris and Mustafa followed him. They started walking up the stairs quietly. On the second floor, Mustafa said: 'This is our apartment.' He tried to open the door but it was locked and he had to knock.

Footsteps approached from the other side the door before a pretty woman opened the door.

'Merhaba[12]. You brought us guests.'

'Yes I did. You know Kemal, and his grandson.'

'Bujrum[13]. What great news. And happy people to come into our home,' said Mustafa's wife cheerfully.

They removed their shoes and put them just inside the door. Mustafa led them to one of the rooms and asked his wife to bring some coffee and cake.

'That's how I tempted them. With your cake!'

They all laughed. 'Esma!' He then looked at his wife 'Is she here?'

'Where else would she be? I'll get her,' Mustafa's wife said.

A few minutes later, a beautiful young woman appeared at the door. She stood next to her father. 'Father you called me?' She looked around the room. 'Selam,' she said, then lowered her eyes and head.

---

12   Merhaba - hello
13   Bujrum – welcome/offer/to serve yourselves

Her long black hair was in a stark contrast to her pale face, which seemed to highlight her beautiful features more. She had warm, brown eyes and small straight nose; her lips were red and full. Haris could not take his gaze off her. When she realised that, she blushed. Kemal looked at her then at Haris, and smiled lightly. Mustafa grabbed his daughter by the wrist. 'We'll have to fatten you up,' he said with a smile.

Esma smiled with embarrassment before mumbling something and turned to go.

'Where are you going? We have guests,' Mustafa said.

'I'll just help Mum.'

As they were drinking coffee, Esma, and Haris were talking quietly together.

'Esma, why don't you show Haris your drawings?' Mustafa said, then turning back to the rest of the group, said: 'Esma draws beautifully.'

Mustafa was obviously quite proud of his daughter's talents. Kemal was bit taken by the thought that this was a good idea. Esma and Haris quite happily went to the other room, and he could hear their conversation begin to flourish.

'I am glad we came here,' Kemal said. 'Esma can really bring Haris out of his melancholia. He is too young to go through all that he has. Inshallah it will not last too long,' Kemal said in one breath.

'I have heard on the radio that presently they are having lots of talks with the Internationals. I believe that an agreement will be reached this time,' Esma's mother said softly.

'She keeps listening to the radio. What we know is that NATO has done the right thing and bombed Republika Srpska or whatever they call it. This should stop the devils,' Mustafa further explained.

'I have heard some news too and now that you say it that way, maybe there is an end fast approaching,' Kemal said.

'Inshallah,' they all said in unison.

After a short pause Kemal said, 'After the occupation finishes, I will go to Mecca with Haris.'

Mustafa and his wife looked at Kemal in astonishment.

'That will be good for Haris. I have never been to Mecca, and I have always wanted to go,' Kemal said. 'If this were to be the last trip of my life, I will die happy.'

When Kemal and Haris returned home, they were all quiet. 'Haris when do you need to go back to your unit?' Kemal finally inquired.

'I need to let the command know that I am back,' he said.

'They surely know that you have been exchanged,' Kemal said with certainty.

'They do,' Haris said with a nod. 'But, I still need to call them, otherwise they will think I deserted.'

'I've heard on the radio today that the presidents are to go to America to sign agreements,' Selma said.

'This war is finished, but the new one then starts,' Kemal said. 'We will have to learn to live with what we have created.'

The phone rang at that moment and Haris answered. 'Hello. Hi... It is me... Yes, sure. I will... No, I had a good time... Well, hmm, thanks for the call. Talk to you soon.' Haris put the phone down and returned to the lounge room.

'Who was that?' Selma asked, surprised that Haris has somebody to talk to so soon after he arrived home.

'Esma. Babo[14] and I met this girl at the mosque. Actually, not at the mosque. We went for a cake to her place.'

Selma looked at Kemal. 'What is he talking about?'

Kemal smiled for the first time since the war started. 'I'll tell you later.' Then he turned to Haris. 'You took a shine to, what's her name...'

'Esma is her name,' Haris said seriously.

Kemal made a face at Selma and whispered. 'I think he is in love.'

Selma smiled too. 'Good.' Then she went to the bedroom and lay down on the bed staring at the ceiling.

Kemal followed her and sat next to her. 'Selma I will turn earth and sky to find him. You must trust me.'

Selma stared at Kemal and said quietly, 'I know.'

A year later Kemal, Selma and Haris were back together in their apartment.

'Are you really sure that you want to do this, Babo?'

Kemal looked at his daughter-in-law. 'Are you out of your mind? Of course I am sure. Now help me. Do we have passports? Where is Haris?'

---

14   Babo - term of endearment for grandfather in Muslim families

'He is on the phone to Esma,' Selma said.

'Haris,' Kemal called. 'We are only going for ten days. You will see Esma when we come back. We have to catch a bus to the airport.'

Selma let a tear drop down her face as she stood at the door. Kemal stroked her head. 'When we come back we will start to look for his remains again,' Kemal said softly.

'You just look after yourself,' she told him, then she hugged Haris and said quietly. 'Look after Babo, he is old.'

'I know, Mum. You look after yourself. If Esma calls—'

'Don't worry I'll tell her that you miss her.' Then she looked at Kemal. 'Call me when you get there just so that I know.'

'Okay, we will. Look after yourself,' Kemal said then he turned to Haris 'Let's go, take that suitcase. Wait for me in the front.'

He then turned to Selma and ushered her in. 'We need to have talk,' Kemal assumed serious look.' You're still young, I don't want you to waste your life with me. Haris is all grown, he doesn't need you.'

Selma's stared in fright. 'What are you saying?'

Kemal touched her head. 'I'm saying, I want you to have a good husband who will look after you,' Kemal said quietly.

'I don't want that. Seid was my husband and still is.' Selma's brow creased.

'He's gone. A woman without a man is open to any abuse. I won't be around for long—'

'I don't need that. I will live with my memories,' Selma said, her lips tight after the last word.

'Fine. But if you do find somebody, I will not blame you,' Kemal said softly.

Selma took a few steps towards the front door, opened it, and then stopped holding the door knob. Kemal shrugged then waved at Selma, as she closed the door.

The apartment felt empty, and she walked from one room to the other as if in a dream. 'What has become of my life?' Her eyes welled with tears as she sat down on the couch. There was a hint of a smile on her face as she looked at the framed photograph of her son and husband displayed in the cabinet. She stood and took a cloth.

She dusted the glass on the framed photograph, kissed it and put it back with tenderness.

Melbourne, Australia, 2000s

Tanya looked around her room: all her summer clothes were spread across her bed and a few pairs of shoes were piled next to the suitcase. Passport. She searched everywhere before finally remembering she'd hidden it in a box at the back of the wardrobe with the rest of her important documents.

She then gathered herself and started calmly putting her clothes into a suitcase. It did not take her long, and after she had finished the job Tanya felt more in control.

She went and had a shower and then set her alarm clock for six o'clock in the morning as her plane was at eleven.

Tanya gave the customs officer a tired smile as she handed over her passport. Once on the plane she fiddled with TV, checked the menu then closed her eyes hoping to fall asleep.

No such luck, so she took out her book and after reading few pages put it away and closed her eyes again.

As she disembarked in Zagreb, she caught a bus to the main bus station where she sat patiently to wait for another bus to take her over the border to Bosnia.

As she waited, she noticed how drastically things had changed. Some poor people were collecting empty bottles, obviously intent on selling them on for a pittance that would then help them survive another day. Things were different when it came to communism; such sights were incomprehensible. Nobody was hungry.

Still the rest of the people at the station seemed to be more in tune with capitalism... or whatever these new times were supposed to be.

Newsagents were filled with glossy magazines, and there was a pride oozing out wherever she looked: "we are part of Europe. We made it." It seemed to say.

Tanya's mother looked even older than she remembered. Small and wiry, her hair was greyer and her hands large on tiny arms. She looked like a grandmother... a grandmother Tanya just couldn't seem to make her mother.

'Do you want to eat something? I've made strudel; you like that. No. First have some lunch,' her mother said fussing over her and walking around the kitchen trying to work out what to bring out first.

'Mum, I ate like a pig on the plane. Sit down and talk. What's the news?' Tanya grabbed her mother by the arm and pulled her to sit down. 'That's nice. Where did you get it?' Tanya stood and looked at the nice fruit bowl on the table.

'Neighbours gave me for Mother's Day,' her mother said.

Tanya slumped back into the seat. 'I'm sorry I wasn't here to give you something for Mother's Day,' Tanya said feeling deflated.

Mother was still fussing around, opening the fridge and putting food on the table, she did not seem to have heard Tanya.

'So what's the news? Who are the neighbours? Are they new?' Tanya asked with renewed vigour.

'There is a woman and her son, Momir, living next door to us,' her mother said. They are from Sarajevo. He works for the International Organization, one of their agencies. There are lots of them around.' Mother assumed a confused look but then continued. 'You should come back to Bosnia, and you will get a job in no time.'

'Mum, my life is there. What else is new?'

'That man is nice. I think he is about your age or thereabout,' her mother persisted.

'Which man?' Then Tanya remembered they were talking about neighbours. 'Mum, no.'

'Well, that's you. Always not interested. How will you marry then?' Sadness pulled at her mother's features.

Tanya hugged her. 'I will marry. I'll do my best.' That discomfort rose from within again – Tanya's inability to do something for the woman who loved her unconditionally. 'I will, I promise.'

Tanya felt she needed a good night's sleep after hours of travel, but the excitement of talking to her mother, being in familiar surrounding was just as tempting. They talked until late that night.

Tanya woke to the smell of freshly-ground coffee and rose with the vigour only this place brought her.

'You're up,' said her mother. 'Good, I just made coffee. Sit here. Do you want to eat something first?'

'Mum, I will have coffee and then I'll have breakfast. What's the time? Nine. Good God, have I slept that long?'

'I did not want to wake you,' her mother said.

'You did well. I needed the sleep,' Tanya said, smiling at her mother.

'I met the neighbours across the landing.'

'Oh, the one that helps with fixing—'

'The other day he came to fix the blocked drain, and he said: "now hold this coil" and he pushed the wire down and he had his back to me, and kept telling me to 'keep unwinding' but it was not fast enough so he got angry with me,' her mother said with a laugh.

A feeling of warmth enveloped Tanya and for a moment she was saddened that she was not here to hear these stories.

'We need to go to the market today,' her mother said. 'What do you want for lunch? I've got some lovely cheese for you for breakf—'

'Mum. Leave it. We'll make something. What time do you want to go to market?'

'The sooner the better; otherwise it gets too hot. It is becoming very hot here. People say that when NATO bombed us they put something in the air and now nature is different, and the weather—'

'Mum, it is more likely to be global warming rather than NATO implanting something.' Tanya felt in control for a moment, feeling that she could still teach something to somebody. Then she added, 'I think I'll have to go to the shop. Is there still one on the corner?'

'Yes. They are very good. What do you need now? You have everything here.'

'Face cream,' Tanya said. 'I forgot to bring some with me.'

Mum was already up from her settee and heading towards the bathroom. 'Look, I have this face cream. It is really good.'

'Mum, I have to buy few more things. I won't be long.'

Tanya went to the bathroom, then made up her bed and got dressed. 'You look nice, Tanya. Why don't you want to find somebody?'

'I will, Mum, I promise.'

Tanya left the apartment and walked down the stairs that were filled with memories of her childhood – a time when she was skipping down the stairs, and when she knew every family in the building.

Many of these families had moved away long before the war. Croat families would move to Zagreb, Serbian to Belgrade. Families that were originally from Bosnia would move to Sarajevo and Macedonians to Skopje. Those families who were left were the ones that did not have high positions and could not better themselves. Since her father left, Tanya and her mum had dropped into that class. At the entrance to the building, Tanya could see the silhouette of a man against the sunny day. When she opened the heavy metal door to let him in, he turned. He was about forty years of age, he had a chiselled face, black hair streaked with grey, and stubble lined his face.

'Hi,' the man said smiling at Tanya.

She smiled back shyly. 'Do you have the key to the building?' asked Tanya.

'Oh, yes, I live here.'

'Are you Momir?' Tanya asked.

'Yes I am,' he said.

'I am Tanya,' she said. 'You must be our new neighbours.'

Momir walked inside the building and closed the door behind him. They found themselves standing across from each other in the small entrance hall of this concrete sixties-built communist-style building. After the first flight of the stairs there were mailboxes for all the apartments made in metal, a style that was changed in the eighties and was installed exactly the same in all the surrounding buildings, Tanya thought.

'Well, we are not that new,' Momir broke Tanya's travel down the memory lane, 'we've been here for two years now. You live in Australia, don't you?'

'Yes I do.' Tanya nodded.

'Cool. Well, do you go out to town often?' Momir asked.

'I just arrived yesterday.' Tanya smiled.

'Oh, right. Well, how long will you be here?' Momir touched her shoulder.

'Six weeks.' Tanya was reminded of the easiness of conversation comparing it to her Australian socialising. It was refreshing to be back in her hometown.

'Well, then we have to organize to go out for a drink soon. I would love to hear about Australia,' Momir said with a smile.

'Sure.' Although she wasn't sure this was something she should be doing.

'How about tomorrow night?'

'Yes, why not. Have you been here through the whole war?' Tanya asked.

'Yes, but how about we leave that story for some other time.'

'Oh, okay, sure,' Tanya said worrying that she appeared too intrusive. 'See you tomorrow then. Maybe we could meet at the front?'

'Sure, eight pm outside.' Momir smiled and then took for the stairs towards his apartment.

As she was walking towards the shop, Tanya smiled. *Well I got myself a date. Maybe it is not exactly a date, maybe just a friendly neighbourly chat. He is nice. I think Mum mentioned that he was from Sarajevo...?*

'Are you going out?' Mum was pottering around Tanya as if she were a child.

'I am,' said Tanya. 'I told you I was meeting Momir.'

'He is nice. But I don't think that he has a degree. No, I don't rememb—'

'It does not matter, Mum,' said Tanya. 'I am not going to marry him.'

'What's the point of going out with him then?' Mother said, resigned.

'It is just a friendly date,' Tanya explained.

Tanya dressed casually but still tried to impress. She put on her white narrow skirt that showed off her legs and a black tight top. As she walked out of the building, she saw Momir. He looked her up and down and smiled. 'You look nice.'

'Thank you.' Momir had shaved and looked younger, although there were still a few lines around his mouth, and his face was drawn in and Tanya blurted out: 'You look like a monk in civilian clothes.'

Momir looked at her in disbelief. 'Whatever. Is there a place where you want to go?'

'No, you lead the way. I am new here in a way,' Tanya said, embarrassed at her silly comment. 'Do you miss Sarajevo?' she asked quietly.

'No,' Momir said shortly, then added obviously trying hard to be patient. 'It is very different now to what it was like when I was growing up.'

'I see.'

'Do you like Australia? Which city do you live in?' Momir asked.

Tanya again had difficulty relaxing, as if something was holding her back from just being in the moment. She looked at him as he was talking and she tried to find him attractive. He had nice straight nose; his Sarajevo accent was very amusing, he had some simple charm that was endearing.

'I'll have a beer. Thanks.' Momir ordered his drink and as waitress left their table Tanya thought that now comes the hard part.

'Was it difficult in Sarajevo during the siege?' Tanya asked.

'I don't really like to talk about that,' Momir said, his words clipped.

'Mum told me that you work for the International Organization. Is it good?'

'Absolutely. That is the best bit. Money is very good. You travel around villages and get stuck in the mud. It is great.' They both laughed. 'Do you work in Melbourne?' Momir asked.

'Not at the moment. I had a job in travel agency, but they closed down. I am supposed to start another job at a library when I return. That will be good.'

'Do you like working in the library?' Momir sipped beer from the glass and then replaced it on the table.

'I have majored in Serbian, and I have always enjoyed books and reading. Yes, I like libraries.' Tanya smiled softly.

'I don't remember the last time I read a book.'

'I read a lot,' Tanya said.

Momir finished his beer and ordered another one. 'Would you like something else?'

'No, I have not finished this first one yet,' Tanya said.

They walked back to their building. He opened the door, and as they walked up the stairs they reached Tanya's apartment. 'Well, sleep well and let's have another drink again soon.'

'Yes, why not. Thanks for tonight I had fun.' She smiled at Momir then went into the apartment quietly. Although it was not too late, her mother was in the habit of going to bed early and Tanya didn't want to wake her.

Tanya went to the kitchen and sat on the settee going over the night in her mind. Something was missing, like it always seemed to be when she went out. Slow footsteps sounded in the corridor.

'Tanya, why don't you go to bed?'

'I will in a moment.' Tanya observed moonlight casting a shadow onto a kitchen bench as it had when she was small.

Mother sat on the settee next to Tanya. 'Did you have good time?'

'It was good.'

'But it wasn't very good. I told you, he doesn't have degree. It is difficult for you with your Masters education.'

Tanya was lost in her thoughts. She felt divided. In some ways she had reached the high points of education and independence, but in other areas she was lacking miserably. Maybe her mother was right; maybe she should find somebody with a degree. But her heart was empty. Her thoughts were empty. Her will was flat. What was the answer?

She met with Momir a few more times. Every time they met he seemed to have been busy with trips with his work or going to parties with his international friends to which he half-heartedly invited Tanya but she declined.

Her six weeks were up very soon and the hard moment of parting with her mother was drawing near. Tanya hated these goodbyes. Her mother would just stand there as if the last drop of blood was drawn out of her body.

Tanya thought that even a wave was an effort of incomprehensible magnitude that Mum's poor body was just about managing to perform.

Tears welled in Tanya's eyes as she turned away from the window of the bus that took her away from her Mother back to Australia, the land of great opportunities and sorrows for people like herself regardless of their nation.

London, UK, late 1990s

Ian returned home looking forward to having a quiet night in with Carol. As he opened the front door of the building Carol was on the phone in the foyer. She waved at him and then said into the phone: 'Okay, I have to go now... Well, okay, we'll talk soon.'

'Who was that?' Ian asked.

'What? Are you my policeman now?' said Carol coming up to him and playfully smacking his bum as she kissed him. 'It was Sarah on the phone, she and Gary are arguing if they should buy and apartment together. Boring!'

'Listen, I've been thinking... What do you think if we buy an apartment or house together?' Ian said as he was walking up the stairs to their bedsit. When he opened the door, he threw his rucksack to the first empty spot he could see. 'I mean this is just too small for us.'

Carol looked around. 'Hmm. You think you and I should buy a place together?'

'No, you and our neighbour,' he said with a laugh. 'Of course you and I.' Ian looked at Carol 'You've gone all red in the face? I mean, you are blushing.'

'Let's think about this.' Carol's nose crinkled as she pouted.

Ian let that go without a word and went to the kitchenette to put the kettle on. The phone rang and Ian turned to the door. 'I'll get it,' he said.

Carol was already out the door and running down the stairs. 'Don't worry I'm used to this by now,' Ian heard Carol say as she reached to the phone.

'Oh, hello Gina. Yes he's here. I'll get him.'

Ian was already walking down the stairs when Carol called out, 'It's for you.'

'Hi Gina, what's up? What trouble have you brewed up this time?... You are?... Why?...Are you sure? Have you spoken with your parents?... Of course you have... I know I am being stupid... Well, don't go without saying goodb... I know you won't.... Okay then. Bye for now. 'Ian put the phone down and returned to the bedsit.

'Gina's leaving,' he said.

Carol frowned. 'Leaving where?'

'She's going back to Bosnia.'

'But why?' Carol asked, her frown deepening. 'Isn't she better off here?'

'I don't know. Maybe she isn't.'

Ian felt a stare on him and he turned to glance at Carol. 'Are you okay?' he asked.

'Yeah,' she said, then after a short pause she added. 'Let's go on holiday somewhere and then we could go to Sarajevo. I would love to see that town.'

Ian was taken aback, then he slouched back on the couch. 'That's not a bad idea,' he said, his gaze wandering around the room. 'But I cannot travel outside the UK until my resident papers are settled.'

'Let's get married then,' Carol jumped off her seat and sat on the floor in front of Ian putting her head into his lap.

Ian's eyes widened, he felt his heart race, his lips curved into smile, he put his hand into Carol's thick hair, brought her head up and kissed her. Carol responded. Ian then pushed Carol's head back gently. 'That's a very big decision. Do you really want to see Sarajevo that badly?' Ian stared at Carol.

Carol stood and then sat next to Ian holding his hand. 'Don't talk crap. I want you to know that I feel very comfortable with you, like I haven't felt with anybody else.' Carol's eyes sparkled, her small upturned nose danced with every breath she took.

Ian stroked her head and continued following her hair line and then held her shoulder in his grip. 'You ground me, you give me strength; you stand out from all that I had before.'

Carol took a deep breath. 'If that's not worthy of commitment, I don't know what is.'

'But do you love me?' Ian stared into Carol's eyes, then held her head in his hands, forcing her to look at him.

'I do,' she said.

Ian kissed her gently and then pulled her closer to him. 'I would like nothing more than to be with you, Carol.'

Carol released herself from Ian's grip, cocked her head, 'And...?

'I love you too, let's do it.'

Gina

Gina was glad to be on the plane. Ian had accompanied her to the airport and helped her buy the ticket. That was the least he could do for her. He had always only looked after himself. Her troubles were never of any concern to him.

She walked away without saying goodbye – he didn't deserve it. She just wanted to be with her parents in familiar surroundings. She hated all these false-smiling attendants on the plane serving and pretending to care.

She was happy to be at the Zagreb airport and although she knew there was another three-hour bus ride to Banja Luka, at least people here spoke her language.

When she arrived at the bus station she began searching for her mother and finally noticed her near the entrance. She looked much older than when Gina saw her last. Her mother opened her arms and held Gina tight. She could feel her mother's bony ribs as she looked over the mother's shoulder at her father. His shoulders were drawn and his hair was completely white.

'Dad, aren't you glad to see me?' said Gina as she threw her arms around him.

'Of course I am. It is just, it is bad here.'

'Just as long as I am with you.' Gina was delighted. 'Mum, did you make my favourite pie?'

'Of course I did. This morning,' her mother answered.

They walked to her father's car. 'You still have your old Ford?' Gina said with a smile.

'What am I going to buy a new one with?' her father said.

Gina was surprised at how little had changed in their apartment. Just that stuff and furniture got older.

'I'll just have a shower and then get stuck into the pie.' Gina walked towards her room 'My room is still the same, too. Lovely.' Gina threw herself on her bed. She lay down for few moments and then went to the bathroom. When she came out there was a baking dish with freshly baked pie waiting for her in the kitchen.

One piece was missing, it was placed on a plate for Gina, next to a glass of yoghurt. Gina sat and started eating. 'Mum, the pie is great,' Gina managed to say between bites.

'What are you going to do here?' her father asked.

'Dad, I'll find something.'

'You couldn't find anything in London, but you'll find something here,' Father mumbled.

'What did you say?' Gina asked, shovelling another piece of pie into her mouth. 'Mum, this pie was worth leaving London for.'

'I am glad you like it, Gina.'

'You know Ian, Mum?' Gina took a last sip of yoghurt and picked few miniscule flakes of pie and put it into her mouth. 'Well, he told me that his friend Momir now lives here and he works for an International Organisation. I can speak English and he might be able to help me get a job.' Gina snuggled next to her mum.

'Let's see that miracle,' Father mumbled again.

'What did you say?' Gina said, but not getting any answer she turned to her mother and carried on. 'Ian has an English girlfriend and he thinks that he is successful because of that. How pathetic!'

'Well, he helped you with putting you in touch with that guy that works with the internationals,' Father said.

'He hasn't helped me. He's just told me about him. Fine I won't get in touch with Momir.'

Mother looked punishingly at Father. 'Don't listen to him. You just get in touch with Momir. You'll get through it yourself. I know you are a good girl.'

'Girl of thirty-four,' Father muttered as he went to the lounge room to watch the news.

'Don't worry about him. This war has really pulled the worst out of him.' Mother looked lovingly at Gina.

Gina felt anguish rise within her. She went to the lounge room and stood in front of her father. He had a surprised look in his face. Gina felt as if all her fears and paranoia were collected in a ball in her throat, she could hardly breathe.

'Look at me! I am what you made me to be. I am your creation. If I am a failure, it is because you failed with me.'

Father's eyes widened slightly as Gina continued.

'Try and get over yourself and take consequences for your actions. You are not an innocent observer. Your derogatory remarks that I am not good enough do not work here! You were looked after by the State, you had a seven to three job. Those times are gone. You wouldn't last a minute in this system. There is no Tito to look after you!'

Gina felt her heart race, she turned around and saw her mother stand in the doorway with her hands clutched across her mouth. 'Gina, neighbours will hear you!'

Gina waved her hand in dismissal. She looked at her father who placed the remote control on the coffee table then went to the window, his back turned. He glanced at Gina, then looked at the picture on the wall, then at Gina again.

Gina stood waiting, her mind clearing slowly.

'I never said that you're a failure,' Father finally said softly. 'I didn't choose my words, I guess,' his head fell for a fleeting moment, then he lifted it up. 'I just want you to be happy.'

'Are you happy?' Gina asked staring at her father's sombre face.

Father approached Gina and took her in his arms, breaking her faint effort to release herself. He held her in a strong embrace and whispered into her ear. 'I would give anything for your happiness. It hurts me to see you being different than the rest. It's a hard way to be.'

Gina felt tears rolling down her cheek, she pressed harder into her father's chest. *There, comfort, finally.* Then she quietly said: 'I know.'

Banja Luka, Bosnia, late 1990s

'So tell me, how's Ian? What does he look like now?' Momir asked.

'He is okay. He has some grey hair, a few wrinkles. Since I met him in London he's put a bit of a weight on. He has an English girlfriend Carol. She's a piece of work.'

'He's always liked them ones,' said Momir laughing with Gina. 'How do you know Ian?'

'His grandparents lived here. We've known each other since childhood. And you?'

'He was my neighbour in Sarajevo,' Momir said and then went quiet.

'That still hurts you?' Gina felt Momir's sombreness.

'It was tough, I won't deny it,' said Momir letting out a sigh.

'It was tough in London, too. You don't have anybody to support you. Even if you are short of a few pounds for rent you have to make that money somehow. Here at least people speak your language.'

'Do we really speak the same language here in Bosnia?' Momir asked.

'True. This café is new,' said Gina looking around. 'You could find something like this in London.'

'Well, it is called "British pub",' said Momir, then added. 'Were you friends with Celine?'

'Why do you ask?' Gina tilted her head.

'Ian mentioned her few times,' Momir said.

'Celine's a bit of a handful. Snake,' Gina said lifting her eyebrow.

'Ian told me that she had a baby with some English guy? But apparently a few months after that, another woman gave birth to his child, too.' Momir took a sip of his beer.

'I don't know anything about that other woman,' said Gina. 'I do know that Celine and her daughter, who'd now be about two, live in an expensive area of London—'

'Mayfair,' Momir said.

'Yes, I think you're right. How do you know that?' Gina stared at Momir in surprise.

'Ian told me. Apparently the flat is in Celine's name and she is the man's de facto and therefore has better 'position' than the other woman,' Momir recalled.

'But who is the other woman? Where did he get her from?'

'Charle... Carly... someth—'

'Charlotte,' Gina smiled.

'Yes, that's it! Charlotte,' Momir lightened up, mystery resolved. 'Do you know her?'

'No, but I believe she replaced Celine in her job when Celine went on maternity leave,' Gina explained.

'Celine is in a bit of a kafuffle?' Momir looked at Gina for a sign of approval.

'She'll be fine. Actually just before I left to come back here, Ian told me she was getting married to Mark,' Gina glanced across the beer garden they were sitting in, then added. 'By the way, she didn't invite Ian to the wedding.'

Momir lifted his hands, palms up: 'Why?'

'Apparently, only close friends were invited, people from the publishing company where they met,' Gina added while pouting her lips and lightly shaking her head. They both laughed before Gina added: 'Whatever.'

Gina looked around the beer garden. Momir took a sip of his beer. 'I met a woman called Tanya, do you know her?'

'Tanya?' A passing shadow covered Gina's face. 'I know her.' Gina's eyes sparkled. 'Where did you meet her? Oh, of course, your flat is in the same building as hers.'

'So you know her?' Momir asked.

'I do know Tanya, she was few years ahead of me in high school. I haven't seen her for ages. She was in London and then came back here and then—'

'She lives in Australia,' Momir said.

'She does?' Gina paused for a moment. 'I guess she hasn't married?'

'No, I don't believe so. What is she like?' Momir asked.

'I think she's always had issues with relationships,' Gina said.

'She lives with her mother. Has her father died?' Momir inquired further.

'No, her parents are divorced.' Gina stopped for a moment, her eyes squinted, 'I don't remember her father ever been around even when we were kids.' Momir's face darkened for a moment, Gina glanced at him and said, 'Do you fancy her? She's okay—'

'No, she looks good and she's... not stupid, but I don't think there was much of a spark between us,' he leaned back into his chair and crossed his ankles.

'How's your work?' Gina leaned forward putting both her elbows on to the table. 'Do you think I could get something at your work place? I am desperate for a job.'

'I think you should be able to find something. How long were you in London?'

'Six years.' Gina focussed her gaze on Momir.

'And you have done some English at school?' Momir lifted his eyebrows.

'Yes.'

'I guess you'll have papers to show that?' Gina nodded 'Then I might be able to help you.'

Gina leaned back into her chair and they went quiet observing the passers-by. It had been three years since the war finished and life seemed to be going back to normal. Everybody called it a transition period – Bosnia was in transition and the transition was to a market economy.

There were lots of makeshift tables all over the town. Even a few Chinese came from their far land to look for work with their one-dollar products. Word of mouth on a world basis. The word was that Bosnia was full of internationals so there was money to be earned.

Some girls came from Eastern countries also looking for work. Internationals were making good money as they were paid for their important efforts to rebuild the country. And as they had to be away from home, they were to be rewarded properly. Local authorities were divided, some were eager to help the internationals as this reflected on them as being seen as forward thinking. Others still behaved as if they were in the throes of war and they wanted to keep the nation and its pride safe.

'I like early autumn here, it's quite mild,' Gina said.

'What was the weather like in London… I mean apart from the rain?' Momir asked.

'London is a big town and there are so many buildings that are hundreds of years old. There are just so many buildings and asphalt everywhere, and you travel mainly on the tube, which is enclosed, so you really don't notice the weather. It is always the same.'

'That's bit boring,' Momir observed.

'That's very boring!' Gina laughed, 'I am glad I am here. I am really pleased to be back. Regardless of this hard situation there is nothing like home.'

'If you have a home,' Momir whispered.

'But you have home?'

'I do,' Momir said. 'Mother and I bought an apartment. It was a lucky chance.'

'That's good. You have somewhere to live. You have a job. What more do you need in life?' Gina gazed at Momir.

'I need what we had before. Friendships, jobs, reasonable prosperity. A sense that I am going somewhere.' Momir gazed into the distance.

'You don't have that now?' Gina asked.

'No, we don't have that. And I believe that it will get even worse. The internationals won't always be here. The government is corrupt. Jobs will not be created. There isn't one big industry that we used to have that is working now. The government will not help open that unless there is lots of money for them to make.'

'That sounds a bit pessimistic,' Gina observed.

'It was easy in the war. You had something to fight against. There was a designed plan that you follow, or as in my case, survive and not been found out. But what do you follow now if you don't have money in your hands?'

'Well, you make money,' Gina snapped.

'How? You can't create something out of nothing,' Momir said.

'If I am good at something and you are also good at something, then we put those two goods together and we start a business,' Gina said logically.

'Are you being serious? What are you good at?' Momir lifted his arms and rested both his palms on his head.

'Hmm, I am good at… cleaning, I can speak English—'

'Is that it?' Momir sneered.

'What are you good at?' Gina said.

'I never said I was good at anything,' Momir said.

'You can drive,' Gina told him.

'I can drive, I can speak a bit of English,' Momir lowered his hands and reached for his beer.

'So with your driving, my cleaning, and both of us speaking English we can open a car wash shop for internationals,' Gina said laughing.

'That is funny,' Momir brushed his lip with the back of his hand and smiled.

'There is always a sunny day after a long night. Dawn breaks regardless,' Gina said, nodding. 'And look we made friends. Friends for life.' Gina twisted her hands, palms up.

'True. Friends for life.' Momir smiled too.

Momir called the waiter, paid for their drinks and then they took a walk through the town that Gina didn't recognise anymore and that was still quite new to Momir. They were in a sense, strangers in their own land.

'I never imagined that my life would be like this,' Gina mused.

'What did you imagine your life would be like?'

'Happier.'

'You were not happy in London either?'

'No. I guess happiness is within you. Will you think about that business we could do together?' Gina asked.

'I will. Maybe we can come up with something that we could both be happy with.' Momir nodded. There was a look of confidence on his face. 'Maybe we can make it work.' He gazed at Gina. 'Why were you so unhappy in London?'

'I was actually developing paranoia. I guess because you feel very lonely there... although I had friends. All I can say is it was tough. Do you miss Sarajevo?'

'The Sarajevo that I knew does not exist anymore,' he said, his lips tightening.

'Neither does Banja Luka,' Gina added.

Momir stared at Gina. 'I guess you are right.'

'For the first time in my life,' Gina mumbled.

'What did you say?' said Momir, but then a man dressed in a full Chetnik uniform attracted his attention. Momir nudged Gina to draw her attention at the man in uniform. Gina was already staring at this man with large white woollen peasant hat, old kingdom of Serbia-style uniform and a crude leather waistcoat.

'He looks like something from a different era,' Gina observed.

'Would we all have been happier if Tito didn't win and there were more people like this?' Momir said more to himself than to Gina.

'I don't understand,' Gina said, a puzzled look on her face.

'That's normal. Us men, we are more clever than you,' Momir said with a cheeky laugh.

Gina rolled her eyes and laughed too.

ACKNOWLEDGMENTS

I would like to thank my family for giving me an upbringing that has shaped me into the person I am today, for better or worse.

I would like to thank each of my friends for giving me occasional guidance along the way that has made me believe that all the struggles are worth it.

I would like to thank my teacher, Julie Postance for having unwavering belief in each of her students and giving us strength to carry this through.

ABOUT THE AUTHOR

Zorica Kecojevic was born in Bosnia and Hercegovina. Just before the beginning of the war she left Bosnia and moved to London 'temporarily'. This temporary period lasted seven and a half years. After returning to Bosnia, and living there for four years, Zorica decided to emigrate indefinitely. She now lives and works in Melbourne, Australia, temporarily.